THE
STICK
GAME

ALSO BY PETER BOWEN

Long Son
Thunder Horse
Notches
Wolf, No Wolf
Specimen Song
Coyote Wind

Imperial Kelly
Kelly Blue
Yellowstone Kelly

THE
STICK
GAME

A GABRIEL DU PRÉ MYSTERY

Peter Bowen

St. Martin's Minotaur
New York

3 2901 00234 6824

ISBN 0-312-20297-0

First Edition: April 2000

10   9   8   7   6   5   4   3   2   1

. . . for the Sweetgrass Hills . . .

✤ CHAPTER 1 ✤

The night was warm for Montana. Du Pré and Madelaine wandered among the booths, where the traders had sat all day, selling jewelry and clothing and crafts. Some of the traders were boxing their things up and taking down the folding display stands.

The Crow Fair at the agency. A bleak town in a third world nation in the United States. The Crows had fought with and scouted for the whites. They had little choice, stuck between the powerful Sioux and the crazy Blackfeet. They were rewarded with some good land south of the Yellowstone and north of the Beartooth Mountains. And the good land was taken by the whites, for cattle, and the Crows shoved east into the hard dry country around the Little Bighorn Battlefield.

"Me," said Madelaine, "I don't want, see them fancy-dancers. I see them fancydancers all the time, always doin' the same thing. Roosters. There is a Stick Game, in that big tent over there, huh?"

Du Pré nodded. The day had been hot. His feet ached from walking around. Alcohol was forbidden at the fairgrounds. He'd run out of Bull Durham and he was smoking pissy tailormade cigarettes that were stale and not good tobacco to begin with.

1

Du Pré was bored.

A big tent made of dark green nylon stood off on a small patch of ground, surrounded by picnic tables. The tables were full of people resting and drinking sodas. Mostly tourists, carrying cameras. Two tables were filled with Japanese, who chattered gaily.

People were spilling out of the front of the big green tent. Du Pré and Madelaine waited until the stream of people thinned and then they made their way inside and over to some bleachers which had a few seats near the top. They climbed up a narrow walk and sat and looked down.

"Kiowas," said Madelaine, "They are pretty good Stick Game players, beat them Sioux, last couple years."

Stick Game, Du Pré thought, this is that. I remember, the one got the bundle of sticks, seventeen or twenty-one, she hold them behind her back and the other team guesses how many she got in each hand. But while they are guessing they got to tell stories, stickholder she tell stories back, sometimes songs. Each story, better than the last.

Three times, the guessing team tells a better story, the stick-holder has to tell them what she got in each hand, they win, or they can guess, try to be lucky.

Tough game.

I think that is how I remember it is played.

Hard to tell, I don't talk Kiowa so good. Kiowa, they say they are Apaches some, never went up into the mountains, stay on the Staked Plains. They were cannibals, like them Sioux and Comanches.

There was a lot of money piled to one side of the players, one for the game, another for side bets, and then there were the real side bets going on between pairs of spectators. Illegal gambling but the State of Montana was a little smarter than trying to bust a Stick Game in the middle of Crow Fair.

Maybe they are that smart, Du Pré thought, though I see them do plenty that is not very smart.

"Du Pré!" said Madelaine, "That is Jeanne Bouyer there! She is my cousin! I have not seen her, maybe ten years!"

Half them people on earth, Madelaine's cousins, Du Pré thought. Chinese cousins. Russian cousins, cousins, Switzerland. Woman has more damn cousins than them Martins got *sheep*.

The Kiowas were guessing. Suddenly one Kiowa woman, a big stately woman in a green beaded cape, stood up and she began to sing a song and tell a story with her hands. She made a snatching motion.

The Gros Ventré team was defeated. The stickholder laid down the two bundles of sticks. The Kiowa women picked up the money piled to the side and in the crowd people were digging in purses or pockets for money and handing it over to people who looked much happier than the diggers were.

"Must have been a good story," said Madelaine, "That Kiowa she just take the Gros Ventré right out of the air, there."

Take the contest.

Du Pré snorted.

"We go see Jeanne," said Madelaine, "I know you are bored, we see her a minute, then we go and get you a drink, Du Pré."

Du Pré followed Madelaine down the steps of the bleachers and through the crowd, which was milling and talking loudly.

Madelaine caught up to her cousin, who was standing with the other three women on the Gros Ventré team. They were all smiling sadly and shaking their heads.

"Jeanne!" said Madelaine. She dragged Du Pré forward by the hand. "How are you, your babies? Your husband?"

Jeanne looked at Madelaine for a moment and then she recognized her and she smiled.

"Ho!" she said, "It is that Madelaine!"

They hugged.

"I am fine. My husband, he was a shit, so I divorce him. Go off to Minneapolis, go to school, but I don't like it there. My babies are . . . they are pretty good. I guess."

Du Pré looked away while the women talked.

When Madelaine pulled him forward to be introduced he smiled.

"Du Pré," said Jeanne, "You be good, my friend Madelaine, I kick your ass you are not."

"She kick my ass I am not," said Du Pré, "So you don't got to help. Worry, either."

"Uh," said Jeanne. She was tall and a little heavy, with a wide smooth face and black eyes. Her hair was braided and the ends of the braids were wrapped with otter skin. She had on some heavy silver bracelets and a choker of buffalo bone and trade beads, black, white, and red.

"Them Kiowa they are tough," said Jeanne, "That was a hard game. But we are better, maybe, next time."

Two other teams had faced off on the blankets and the songs were starting. The air in the tent was close. Du Pré wanted a cigarette.

"Du Pré," said Madelaine, "She meet us, downtown, the bar there that is the Stockman, huh?"

"Ok," said Du Pré. Relief.

"Yah," said Jeanne, "I want to get rid, some of this jewelry, maybe go down, have a cheeseburger."

"A beer," said Du Pré.

"I don't drink alcohol no more," said Jeanne.

Jeanne went off toward a small door in the back of the big tent. Du Pré and Madelaine pushed their way through the crowd and outside. The air was a little cooler but not that much.

Madelaine took Du Pré's arm and she held close to him.

"My cousin she got something on her mind," said Madelaine.

"Uh," said Du Pré.

"Her kids, they are in trouble some," said Madelaine.

"What she say?" said Du Pré.

"She don't say nothing," said Madelaine, "She don't have to. Women they get that little line between their eyebrows, go up and down, they are worried a lot. She is rid of that shit Gros Ventré she marry, she got that line, so it is her kids."

Du Pré nodded.

Me, I can track a coyote across rocks but not a woman's mind across her forehead, he thought, so that is about right.

"Who is this shit Gros Ventré?" said Du Pré.

"He is that Charley Bouyer. I never like him, he is mean, I see his eyes. He beat her up some, you bet."

Gros Ventré got a Métis name, lots of them Sioux, Crow, whatever. Us Métis, we marry anybody, Du Pré thought, they still don't like us much. That Charley Bouyer I know him, can't remember.

They walked through the parked cars to Du Pré's old police cruiser, shorn of the light bar and siren but still very fast. They got in and drove to downtown Hardin and found the Stockman and they went on in.

The bar had been recently redone and it smelled of disinfectant. The floor was quarry tile and the bartop was thick plastic over wood. The walls still held yellowed photographs of ranchers, mostly white. There were branding irons and a pair of dried-out shotgun chaps and the usual ratty antelope heads mounted on slabs of oak, with brass plates to tell who had shot them.

A stuffed javelina on a shelf over the old nickel-plated cash register, and a stuffed longhorn head. The longhorn head was pretty new and hadn't lost much hair yet.

Du Pré ordered a whiskey ditch for himself and some sweet wine for Madelaine. The cheerful woman behind the bar mixed the drinks and she took Du Pré's money and she gave him change and Du Pré left a dollar on the bartop for a tip.

They drank and waited for Jeanne Bouyer.

They danced for a while.

After two hours they looked at each other.

"I don't think that she will come," said Du Pré.

Madelaine shook her head.

"It is her kids," she said.

The drove to the motel and watched television for a while before going to bed.

✤ CHAPTER 2 ✤

Du Pré was fiddling with some Turtle Mountain people. They were on stage in Calgary, one of several stages set up on the park grounds. People could wander and find an act that they liked and then sit and hear it and go on.

There were hawkers of fruit juices and snacks wandering in front of the stage.

Du Pré was very thirsty and he wished the song would end in time for him to snag one of the hawkers and get a cool drink. But by the time the song ended the hawkers were too far away.

Du Pré and the Turtle Mountain people finished their set and took a break and they went to the edge of the stage and cased their instruments while an old-timey band of bearded college types set up.

"Pret' good playin'," said Bassman. He slipped a chamois cover over the fretless electric bass he had made himself.

"Yah," said Du Pré "You lay up that good floor there."

Bassman nodded. He was a fine bass player, subtle, always proving a steady beat and rhythm for the violin and guitar to lift up from. He was Du Pré's cousin. They had been playing together off and on for nearly forty years.

"You know," said Du Pré, "I been playin' with that Tally,

him on the accordion, long time, I don't know what happen to his legs."

Tally's legs were twisted and he had a bad back. He used crutches to get from place to place, though he could manage to stump for short distances, his head thrown way back to keep his balance.

"Born that way," said Bassman, "His mother she is in Ontario when she is pregnant with him. Her husband he is working in the smelter at Sudbury. They are poor, she gets some bad water, had something in it. Lots of kids there are crippled, some of them retarded, they have to be in the hospitals all their lives. Lots of babies born dead, too."

Du Pré nodded:

"Well," he said, "He play that accordion pret' good."

Du Pré lifted his fiddle case, a rawhide one his father had made and his mother had beaded and quilled.

Tally was packing up his accordion. He leaned on one crutch and held the other under his arm and he seated the accordion and closed the lid and flipped the catches and he lifted the heavy case easily and held it against his right crutch and he made for the stairs. He was enormously powerful in the shoulders and arms. Someone made his shirts for him. His neck and upper arms would have burst a storebought shirt at the seams.

"We play again, three hours," said Bassman. He was looking at a schedule. "That Sound Stage seven, right after that lady singer from Texas."

Du Pré nodded.

Du Pré heard the ululations of the Inuit throatsingers in

9

the distance. He grinned. He walked down the steps and made off toward the eerie warbling.

Them Inuit make me think of ice and snow ever'where, they sing, Du Pré thought, pret' cold up there, the Arctic Ocean. Hunting seals. Man want to make his wife happy, he take her a seal liver. Wealth. Me, I would like to go, see where these good people came from.

The Inuit were grouped around a bank of four microphones. The crowd was paying rapt attention. Du Pré stood in the back and he listened hard. The Inuit didn't pause between songs, they would change the tune a little and keep going. After half an hour, they quit.

The people watching clapped hands and they cheered. The Inuit smiled shyly. They were older people, and not used to so many people all in one place. Or trees. He had seen some of them touching the trunk of a maple and looking up at the green leaves with wonder on their faces. At the tents where the performers ate, the Inuit ate salads. Huge salads. They loved salads.

Far north people, tough country. No salads.

Du Pré went to the performers' tent and he found his bag and he fished a plastic bottle out and had a swig of whiskey. It was very expensive in Canada, and you had to go to a Government store to get it.

"We don't sell it in the drugstores," said the clerk, looking at the performer's badge on Du Pré's shirt.

Them tightass English, Du Pré had thought, me, I never like them that much. Got no blood, or something.

There were a couple scarlet-coated Mounties wandering

through the festival. Tall and with moustaches. Keeping the peace.

Du Pré sipped his whiskey and he rolled a cigarette and went on outside, through a door in the back of the tent. There were portable toilets there and a shower enclosure with a pressure tank and a propane water heater. Some of the performers got soaked in sweat, if they were on a stage that faced the sun, the stage gathered heat like a solar oven.

"Hey, Du Pré!" said Tally. Du Pré looked over and down. Tally was less than five feet tall with his crutches, though he had a big head and he was very handsome in his face.

"Good accordion," said Du Pré.

"You are wondering about my legs, eh?" said Tally. He was grinning.

Du Pré was embarrassed. Damn Bassman.

"Bassman don't say nothin'," said Tally, "I just see your face, there, I see a face like that all the time. My mother, she drink bad water and I am born like this. My spine was not covered, down low, it is open to the air. I almost die."

Du Pré nodded.

He looked at Tally's left hand. No ring, he had never married.

"Me," said Tally, "I stay away from them women, don't want one marry me because she pity me. Also, I get infections down there, all the time, I stink sometimes."

Du Pré rolled a cigarette and handed it to him.

"That damn mining company they say they don't know why I am like this, they are so sorry," Tally went on, "But then all these poor people they have babies like me, or sim-

11

ple, or born dead. Too many of them. People don't live near a mine, a smelter, they are all right mostly, this only happens once, a while."

Du Pré nodded.

"I am taking a shower," said Tally, "Had the infection, it is draining again. Maybe you watch my accordion?"

Du Pré nodded. Tally could check his accordion with the security people but he obviously didn't want to.

Tally went inside and he got a bag and went to the shower enclosure and he pulled back the plastic sheet and went in. Du Pré heard the water.

Du Pré had some more whiskey. He waited fifteen minutes and then Tally came out in fresh clothes. He had his bag and a piece of newspaper folded up. He put the newspaper in the trash.

"Thanks," he said. He looked at Du Pré.

"You know, we got our people, Fort Belknap Reservation, got a lot of our people there," Tally said slowly.

Du Pré nodded.

"Some of them kids, a lot of them kids, they are having some trouble in school," said Tally, "So the mining company says, it is not us, our gold mine, it is because they are dumb Indians."

Du Pré nodded.

"Kids got the lowest test scores, whole state of Montana," said Tally, "And they all live, next to the two creeks the mine drains water from."

OK, Du Pré thought, here it comes.

"That mining company, Persephone," said Tally, "It is killing them kids. Might as well. Lots of birth defects, too."

Du Pré waited.

"You good at finding things out, Du Pré," said Tally, "I hear that you are very good, finding things out."

Du Pré nodded.

"The people, State of Montana, supposed to see that the mine don't poison people, they say the water is fine, Du Pré," said Tally, "But if the water is fine, why are the kids so stupid, so many of them?"

Du Pré looked at Tally.

"It is too late for me," said Tally, "But maybe not for them, or the ones not born yet. You maybe go there, look?"

Du Pré shrugged.

"They your people, Du Pré," said Tally. He gripped Du Pré's wrist and he squeezed slowly.

Du Pré looked at him.

"Don't you, break my bones," said Du Pré.

Tally laughed. He let go.

"They are your people, lots of people, Ver'sad," said Tally, "I hear you got a rich friend, he maybe help find out, that water."

Du Pré shrugged. Bart was rich. Of course he would.

"You maybe do this," said Tally, "Not for me, for that music?"

Du Pré grinned.

"OK," he said, "I will go and see."

13

"No," said Tally, "You don't go and see."

Tally's dark eyes were level and full of fire.

"You go and find," he said, "You find, Du Pré. They are killing, your people."

Du Pré nodded.

He had a little more whiskey.

✤ CHAPTER 3 ✤

D u Pré was standing on the slope of one of the low hills near a buffalo jump. The contours of the hills were soft and in places limestone formations weathered out by the chewing waters hugged the little arroyos. It was August and it was damn hot. The grass was ready to burn. If it caught fire it could move, with the right wind, eighty miles an hour.

Down below there was a small archaeological dig. The rancher who owned the land permitted the University of Washington to excavate a site near an old stream that had cut down and filled in and now was just a greener stripe of rank grass winding between old banks.

Long time ago, it ran with a lot of water, Du Pré thought.

He walked back down the hill. A young woman wearing a space suit was washing soil in a box sieve. She sprayed pressured water on the soil that the diggers brought.

Bart was standing with the archaeologist. He was waving his hands.

" . . . send me the published material and I'm sure that the family foundation will consider it," said Bart.

Du Pré snorted. News of Bart's money had run on ahead of him. The archaeologist could use a grant. Bart had enough money to buy any of the world's smaller countries. For cash.

Bart and the professor shook hands and the archaeologist went up toward the young woman in the space suit, his hands in his pockets, head down and thinking.

"Hair," said Bart, "Who'd have thought?"

The dig was after human hair. It didn't rot and people lost about two hundred a day. DNA tests could be run on it. It could be dated. The tools and bones found near the hair had definite dates. Du Pré had been amazed.

"Pity the professional Indians are so intent on controlling it," said Bart, "You know that the digs are only on private land? The Government is so afraid of offending that they buy that crap about this hair being funerary. I suppose they'd do the same thing with dandruff."

"Ah," said Du Pré, "That Bucky Dassault, the asshole, he is now that Benjamin Medicine Eagle? He is hiring himself out, to explain Indian religious beliefs to gold miners."

"Why haven't you just shot the fucker?" said Bart.

Du Pré shrugged. He couldn't think of a good answer.

Why *haven't* I shot the fucker?

No good reason.

"This pretty interesting," said Du Pré.

"People were here," said Bart, "for twelve thousand years. The glaciers missed these hills. For no one knows what reason. Sacred hills. And look at all the tire tracks all over them? Isn't this one of the Indian heavens? You come to the Sweetgrass Hills when you die? And disgusting apes on motorcycles and four-wheel drives tear them up. Why don't they just go to the National Cathedral and crap in it?"

"Oh," said Du Pré, "Well, it has been pret' bad. That damn Mount Rushmore, there, the Black Hills. I never like it."

"Oh, that," said Bart, "Hell, blast it down. It's sure no improvement."

"You damn whites," said Du Pré, "You got to shit on everything, make sure we all know that you're here."

"I ain't white," said Bart, "I'm Italian."

Du Pré nodded.

Big Jim Lascaux and David Stone came up to Bart and Du Pré. Big Jim was a packer and hunting guide. He also had a doctorate in archaeology. Stone was a professor of geology at the school in Bozeman. They were friends of Bart's.

"Pretty amazing," said Stone, "I'll dig out the maps when I get home. But, if what you've said is true, then it does pay out or Persephone would not be at all interested in mining here."

"They admit that in thirty years they will utterly destroy the Sweetgrass Hills," said Bart, "Dig them up, pulverize them, heap-leach the gold out, and walk away. After scattering a little grass seed."

Cyanide leaching could remove minute quantities of gold from rock that had been crushed. Another company was going to dig up Nevada in a strip sixty miles wide and a hundred and fifty miles long.

"Well," said Big Jim Lascaux, "Thanks for coming. Persephone won't start in here for a decade, probably, but you know what these hills mean to archaeologists. There wasn't any ice here. So this is where people lived. Who knows how long ago."

"How long have people been in the New World?" said Bart.

Big Jim shrugged. "On the evidence, thirty thousand years. But during the glacial periods the seas were lower. People could have come down the littoral, that would have been easiest and so they probably did. But there isn't any evidence. The seas rose and washed what may have been there away. This was on the Great North Trail. People coming from Siberia across the Bering Land Bridge would have come through here."

Du Pré nodded.

Them Athapascans, mean fuckers, come down the road from Tibet. Run them damn Sioux east, for sure. Apache, Kiowa, Navajo, Haida. Athapascan.

Shoshones were here a thousand years, though, at least. Me, I got some Shoshone in me.

Big Jim walked away, one of the technicians at the pits dug in the old streambanks was waving to him.

"He never teach, get that good university job?" said Du Pré.

"Hah," said Stone, "Jim is an honest man. Tell you something. Professors are the most dishonest, sleazy bastards on earth. Big Jim would have done murder, about halfway through the first faculty meeting. I can stand it now, I'm tenured, but the asses I had to kiss to get there will leave a bad taste in my mouth for the rest of my life."

Du Pré nodded.

"Big Jim is a legend," said Bart, "He's thrown folks

through walls in most bars in Montana. Threw a guy straight up through a skylight in a yuppie bar in Missoula. Yeah, I like Big Jim. You Montanans all scare the shit out of me, but he flat *terrifies* me."

Du Pré shrugged. Long ago Du Pré's father had killed Bart's brother Gianni. Bart and Du Pré had unraveled the story. Now Du Pré had to admit that if he'd been in Papa Catfoot's moccasins, he would have killed Gianni, too.

Bart knew that.

They were good friends and so did not talk of it.

"I'll send a big check to the dig," said Bart.

"Good," said Stone, "I know these people. They are honest and they are at least determined to do some serious scholarship here."

"But," said Bart, "they are professors."

"I know," said Stone, "It grieves me. We are sluts and whores and we suck up to the rich shamelessly. Like other sluts and whores."

"Yeah," said Bart, "I know."

They grinned at each other.

"Mr. Stone," said Du Pré, "They do this mining, like they are doing over by Zortman, what else. . . . why is the water made bad?"

"There are a lot of other metals down there and the mining either drops them into the water table or the surface streams," said Stone, "Or the cyanide leaches them out and they go from being inert, chemically combined with something and made harmless, to active. Cadmium, selenium, arsenic, lead, antimony, all bad. Heavy metals are bad. They cause illness in adults, they are worse in children, worst of all in the unborn. In Japan, a company was leaking mercury into a bay and the townspeople ate the shellfish and their children were often born horribly deformed."

Du Pré nodded.

"What do they mine, that Sudbury, Ontario?" he said.

"Nickel," said Stone, "But there's a bad brew of other heavy metals along with it."

"OK," said Du Pré, "You are in Bozeman? I have some questions I can maybe call you?"

"Sure," said Stone. "Any time. If I don't know I can find out."

"There's something sad going on on the Fort Belknap Reservation," said Bart, "Kids with bad learning problems. Retardation."

"I know," said Stone.

"How you know, how long?" said Du Pré.

"Since they started," said Stone, "See, what happens is this. The Legislature or the Congress may pass laws about acceptable amounts of pollution from mining. But then the Republicans cut back the budgets so the people who are supposed to keep an eye on the mining companies are all fired for lack of money. It's like passing laws against murder and then shooting all the cops."

Du Pré nodded.

"That's what they do," Stone went on, "and at this rate finding a pure glass of water to drink anywhere in the country will be damned hard by the middle of the next century."

Du Pré nodded. He pulled a leather flask from his hip pocket and he sipped a little whiskey.

He offered the flask to David Stone.

"Don't mind if I do," said Stone. He took the flask and tipped it to his lips.

A little fell on his worn red flannel shirt.

✤ CHAPTER 4 ✤

She call yesterday," said Madelaine. She and Du Pré were lying in bed. He'd gotten back from the Sweetgrass Hills two hours before, and now was the first moment they had had to talk.

"OK," said Du Pré, wondering which she had called.

"Her Danny, he has disappeared. His friends they say that he is gone but they don't know where and they don't see him."

"This is your cousin Jeanne?" said Du Pré.

"Who the hell you think I am talking about, Du Pré?" said Madelaine.

Du Pré looked at the ceiling and he didn't say anything.

Smart man keep his mouth shut except when he is told to open it I think, Du Pré thought, she has been thinking of this Jeanne for some days and she thinks I must have been, too. I will live to be a hundred and not understand these women any better. Just hope they like me OK. Love me and like me OK.

"How old is this Danny?" said Du Pré.

"Sixteen," said Madelaine, "It is a bad age for a boy."

Not so good for dogs, either, Du Pré thought.

"Jeanne she is frantic. Danny, he always has trouble in school. He hangs out with bad young men. He drinks, he takes drugs," said Madelaine.

You have just described nine out of ten sixteen-year-old boys I could find smoking dope in the coulees, ten miles around here. I know all of them. They will probably turn out OK. Me, I am sixteen, I drink a lot of beer, smoke marijuana some. Look at what a great success I am, here. Play the fiddle, look at cow asses, keep finding trouble, Du Pré thought and he kept staring at the ceiling.

"She don't know what to do," said Madelaine.

Du Pré nodded. Me neither.

OK.

"I tell her you come over, maybe look around," said Madelaine.

"WHAT?" said Du Pré. He sat up.

"You hear me," said Madelaine, "She is really worried."

"I am not a cop, Fort Belknap," said Du Pré, "They got cops there know everyone, you know."

"Cops, Fort Belknap don't like Danny. He steals sometimes. They say he run away, he's maybe down in Billings, on the street, Missoula, Great Falls."

Du Pré nodded.

"There is something else," said Madelaine.

Du Pré looked at her.

"I don't know what it is," said Madelaine, "Her voice got something else in it I can't tell."

"OK," said Du Pré, "We drive, Fort Belknap, you talk to

her, I look for Danny. I don't even know what he looks like, anything. She has pictures. If this make you feel all right."

"I always like Jeanne," said Madelaine, "I always like her, she is very kind. She marry that bastard who beat her up, drunk all the time. She go way off to Minneapolis, she study, she get her degree, she come back for some reason she don't tell me."

"OK," said Du Pré, "We go. We go."

"In the morning," said Madelaine.

"In the morning," said Du Pré, "Now, me I want to maybe go down to the bar, have a steak, some drinks, talk to some friends. That Bart he bring back this packer who is an archaeologist, I like him. He looks like a bear. Looks like a bad dude. Tough. Very smart. Most of them, they are not smart at all."

Madelaine nodded.

Du Pré got up and he went down the hall toward the shower. Madelaine's kids spent very little time at home, just to grab some sleep and something to eat, so they were there alone. He went naked.

He stood in the hot shower, whistling.

"Baptiste's Lament."

Need to play my fiddle some. Go see old Benetsee if he is there or that Pelon he is not. Or both of them. Then I got to go to Fort Belknap and find some kid if I can and I don't know he want to be found. People, they got to be able to run. Me, I run to the Army. They send me to Germany. A Métis in Germany. I got soap in my goddamn eyes.

Du Pré ran water in his eyes and they quit burning a little. Madelaine made this soap. It got you very clean, burned off a couple layers skin.

Du Pré got dressed in clean worn old clothes. He waited while Madelaine bathed and put on her long skirt and ribbon blouse and jewelry and she fixed her thick silver-shot black hair. She smelled of flower potpourri. Which she made, from flowers she picked and dried. Then she made soap scented with the potpourri and Du Pré had always loved the way that she smelled.

"So?" said Madelaine, smiling and turning around, "You fuck pret' good, Du Pré, I am a lucky woman, yes."

They walked the four blocks down to the bar. There were a few cars out front and Du Pré saw Bart's big dark blue Land Rover and Sheriff Benny Klein's Jeep with the light bar and siren.

They went in. The place was gloomy at first, and it smelled of cooking meat and spilled beer, cigarette smoke and wet dogs. Bart's two huge Chesapeake retrievers were slumped at his feet, and they had gone swimming in the river recently.

The dogs looked at Du Pré with their yellow eyes and they both gave a slight wag of the tail.

Big Jim Lascaux was talking with Susan Klein, who was laughing and holding her sides. Her laugh boomed out and warmed the room.

Du Pré and Madelaine walked up to Bart and Big Jim and Benny.

Madelaine looked at the three of them.

"You guys, off alone, you have a good time?" she said, "Lots of good time, go to the whorehouse?"

"Twice a day," said Bart, "They have blonde twelve-year-olds. Twins, though they cost more."

"Twelve-year-olds?" said Madelaine, looking at Du Pré, "Hey Du Pré you come here now I want to talk to you . . . "

She was looking at her knuckles.

Susan Klein pushed a ditch and some bubbly pink sweet wine across the bartop and Du Pré reached out and he got Madelaine's wine and he gave it to her.

"The Siamese twins were good, too," said Bart.

"Uh," said Madelaine.

"I think Du Pré is gonna die now," said Big Jim.

"Eh?" said Madelaine, "Men, they are like that."

"This is Big Jim Lascaux," said Du Pré, "This is Madelaine Placquemines."

Big Jim stuck out a hand the size of a plate. Madelaine took it and she grinned at Jim.

"The archaeologist?" she said, "I read some your articles."

"Which ones?" said Big Jim.

"Old stone tools," said Madelaine, "Bart showed me. I know where there are some like that a while ago, but not now."

Big Jim looked at her.

"When?" he said.

"Oh," said Madelaine, "Twent' years ago, you know, we have that bad spring, rain, snow, freeze, floods, that little creek by Bart's flows into Cooper Creek, right there, a bank is washed away, we find a bunch of those tools, me, my sister. I still have them. Bird bones, some old buffalo bones all black from fire."

Big Jim nodded.

"We got to go, Belknap tomorrow," said Madelaine, "But you go out to old Booger Tom, Bart's place, he knows where."

"I have a site on my land and I don't know it?" said Bart.

"Shit," said Madelaine, "You have Willy the Whale on your land you don't know it, Bart, you don't ride it like Booger Tom."

Bart grinned.

"Take my man, the whorehouse, I am mad at you," said Madelaine.

"He wouldn't go," said Bart, "He went to confession."

"What you got to confess, Du Pré?" said Madelaine.

"Twelve-year-old blond twins," said Du Pré.

"Uh," said Madelaine, "You guys getting to old for that. Get there, can't do anything anyway. All wilted."

"What kind of tools?" said Big Jim.

"Scrapers," said Madelaine, "Lots of them big, big spear-points, not so pretty, you know, crude."

Big Jim nodded.

"Also there is this arrowhead making place up there," said Madelaine jerking her head toward the Wolf Mountains.

"A quarry?" said Big Jim.

"Big piece of that black glass," said Madelaine.

"You know where that is?" said Big Jim, looking at Du Pré.

Du Pré shook his head.

"What's a deposit of obsidian doing in the Wolfs?" said Big Jim, "They aren't volcanic."

"Other side," said Madelaine, "Du Pré don't go there much."

"How did you find it?" said Big Jim.

"How you find the whorehouse?" said Madelaine.

Big Jim nodded and he smiled.

✤ CHAPTER 5 ✤

G od damn kid," Jeanne spat. They were sitting in the little kitchen of her Government house, a tiny three-bed-
room modular dwelling much like a trailer without wheels.

"He run off before?" said Madelaine.

Jeanne shook her head.

"It is not like him," she said.

She looked out the back window and she rapped sharply
on the glass.

"Damn dogs shit everywhere but the owner's yard," she
said. Three cats were lying on the counters in the kitchen,
cleaning themselves.

"So this is Danny?" said Du Pré. He was holding a school
picture in a cheap plastic pop-in frame.

"Yah," said Jeanne, "It was taken this last year. He is a little fatter, little taller now, but that still looks like him."

Du Pré stared. Dark complexion, some acne, broad face.
Pretty common face on the res. Du Pré thought he could
remember it.

"Who saw him last?" said Madelaine.

"He was at school, he left before it was over for that
day," said Jeanne, "Some kids saw him walking across the

29

field next to the school and that's the last time anyone saw him."

"When?" said Du Pré.

"Middle of June," said Jeanne.

"That is, maybe, ten weeks ago," said Du Pré. "You talked to the cops?"

"Yah," said Jeanne, "They look around some, call here, there, they don't find nothing. They say he is a runaway, got thousands in the country, we sent his name, picture out. How many Indian kids are out there, you know? They don't look for him very hard. It is easy to hide, too."

"When he left," said Du Pré, "What did you think when you don't come back here, find him?"

"I don't know," said Jeanne, "My boyfriend, he is here, they don't get along anyway, I think he maybe be at his father's. But he is not."

"Where's he?" said Du Pré.

"Half mile," said Jeanne.

"Your other kids, what they say?" said Madelaine.

"They don't know," said Jeanne, "Paulette, she give me this, though."

Jeanne pulled a folded sheet of school notebook paper out of the telephone book. She handed it to Madelaine.

Madelaine read it. It wasn't long.

"He say he is so sad he will kill himself," said Madelaine, "He is sorry but he can't do this no more."

Jeanne nodded.

"He ever talk about doing this before?" said Madelaine.

Jeanne shook her head. No.

"They look all the places to jump off, the places he might have gone. But he don't have a gun, he don't have razor blades, maybe he has dope but there isn't all that much here, we don't got money," said Jeanne.

"The police they know about this?" said Du Pré.

Jeanne shook her head. "I don't show it to them," she said, "Then they call him crazy, put him in Warm Springs maybe."

Du Pré nodded.

"You maybe call one of his friends, let me talk to them?" said Du Pré.

"OK," said Jeanne, "That Jesse, he might talk, you."

She went off to the telephone in her bedroom and she talked for a minute and then she came back.

"He coming over," she said.

Du Pré sipped the bitter instant coffee that Jeanne had made for them. He rolled a cigarette.

"I have one of those?" said Jeanne, "I am quitting, but I want one now."

Du Pré lit it and he handed it to her.

One of the cats, a fat white one, meowed loudly. Jeanne went into the kitchen and she cooed while she petted the cat.

Madelaine looked at Du Pré shaking her head slightly.

Someone knocked at the thin front door. Jeanne walked out to it very slowly and she opened it. There was a skinny kid standing there, baseball hat on backwards, chewing gum.

"This is Jesse," said Jeanne, "This is Du Pré." She pointed at Du Pré, who nodded. "He wants to talk, you."

Du Pré got up and he went to the door. He turned and

jumped to the ground, over the three steps down. He flexed when he landed, and he spread his arms.

"So," said Du Pré, "Jesse, you don't know nothin' 'bout where Danny went?"

Jesse looked at Du Pré. He had a bad eye, offset, looking off at nothing. The other was pretty blank.

He shook his head.

"He ever talk maybe he kill himself?" said Du Pré.

Jesse looked at Du Pré for a moment. Then he nodded.

"He doing drugs?" said Du Pré, "I am not a cop, Jesse, I am trying to find him for his mother."

Jesse didn't answer.

OK, Du Pré thought, I will try this now.

"Look," said Du Pré, "You guys, you are friends, you got to have some place that you go, hang, drink some beer, maybe, smoke some grass. You got a place like that?"

Jesse stared at the ground.

"I don't want, make trouble," said Du Pré, "But I am gonna, you don't quit fucking with me. Jeanne, she is worried some sick. Her son is gone, she don't know where. So what you say."

"We got a place," said Jesse. "It's supposed to be a secret."

Du Pré nodded.

"Danny is not there, no?" he said.

Jesse shook his head.

"You been there, you know that?" said Du Pré.

Jesse looked at Du Pré.

Du Pré grabbed Jesse by the shirt and he jerked the boy over in front of him.

"We are going there," he said, "We go there now. When we get there, I will know it is the right place. It is not, I will kick the shit out of you, you hear me, you little bastard?"

Jesse looked away.

Du Pré dragged him to his old cruiser and he shoved him in and he got in and started the engine.

"Where to?" said Du Pré.

Jesse nodded down the street. Du Pré drove. They got to a corner and Jesse nodded right.

They went about three miles outside of town. When they came to a dirt track leading off through sage toward a ridge knifing up from the yellow prairie Du Pré turned and he drove to the end. The track stopped at a little hidden creek that purled down from a higher ridge three or so miles away.

There was a little hidden basin, down by the creek, and an old plywood trailer surrounded by rank bottoms grass. Trash piles, old enough to be mostly rusty cans, lay at the base of the little drop from the flat field. There were a couple of old car bodies gone to brown rust and a refrigerator, still white, standing upright by a cottonwood stump.

"OK," said Du Pré, "You guys have this. I want to look at it."

Jesse led him down to the trailer. The door was gone and flies hummed inside. Du Pré looked in, saw the torn mattresses and old sleeping bags and the skin magazines. The trailer was small. Not much room. It smelled of mildew.

33

"You guys come out here, eh?" said Du Pré. He looked at a charcoal grill on some cinder blocks half covered with last year's tumbleweeds.

Jesse nodded.

OK, Du Pré thought, them cops they would check this place. I think.

Du Pré walked around the trailer slowly, about thirty feet away from it. He moved through the tall grass and he looked down.

He stumbled over a line of stones. There was a little mortar on them, just stains, old and thin and crumbly.

Du Pré walked around the old foundation. A house had stood here, long ago, the wind had taken everything but the rough foundation.

Root cellar would be over there, in that claybank, then, Du Pré thought. He walked over and then he saw the outline of an old doorway that had been crushed by slippage. The frame was broken down. Du Pré could see black shadow past the reach of the sun.

Du Pré squatted and he looked in. The roof had caved in and there was yellow earth piled deep back about three feet. The old timbers had held the light weight of the front slope up some.

That's been there a long time, Du Pré thought.

Now I find the well.

Du Pré looked at the creek line.

Well up there, outhouse would be down there, he thought.

He walked toward where he thought the well would be.

34

He saw a low stone circular wall, only four feet or so in diameter.

Du Pré walked up to it.

Old gray boards on the top, a thick bolt from a tree.

Got a new piece of rope on it.

Du Pré bent closer and he smelled the sweet, fishy smell of dead humans well rotted.

He straightened up. He walked back to the cruiser. Jesse was sitting inside it.

Du Pré drove back to Jeanne's. Jesse got out and he walked away without saying anything.

Du Pré went on into the house.

❧ CHAPTER 6 ❧

The firefighters were coughing hard. The corpse had come up in pieces and the stink was awful. They had tried to do the job without masks, the day was hot, and just wipe mentholated petroleum jelly in their nostrils, but the stink shot right through.

Du Pré was standing well upwind with a couple Tribal Policemen. Mid-thirties and tough. Dark glasses. Braids.

"Well," said one, "I looked around out here but I didn't think of the damn well."

"Which we would have if Jeanne had showed us the fucking note," said the other.

Henry and Joe. Du Pré couldn't remember their last names though he had just heard them.

"Poor little bastard," said Henry.

One of the doctors from the Indian Health Service was standing by.

"Government even gives us coroners," said Joe, "He ain't gonna like this autopsy."

"Hell," said Henry, "Neither are you. It's your turn."

"Fuck you say," said Joe, "I did it last. . . . oh, Christ, I forgot. Shit."

"Hee hee," said Henry.

36

"Little bastard coulda slashed his wrists and bled to death all nice and clean, I could have handled that," said Joe.

"One more dead Indian kid," said Henry, "I get awful tired of this. Poor little bastards, got no place to be and no place to go."

"Coulda grown up and been one of the elite, like us," said Joe.

"Fucking-a," said Henry, "Real elite. We got *jobs*. We get *paychecks*."

Du Pré sighed. Madelaine was back at Jeanne's, comforting.

Me, I am standing here while they pick up her rotten kid. Not funny.

"Pret' good thinking, Du Pré," said Henry, "How you know to do this?"

Du Pré shrugged. He hadn't thought of it till he'd met Jesse. Jesse was behind the three of them, on his hands and knees, vomiting. He'd gotten curious, and walked up to the well just when the firefighters had heaved a big piece of Danny out.

Du Pré looked at the doctor, in his white lab coat. The young man was standing with his arms across his chest. He reached up his hand and took off his dark glasses and he rubbed his eyes.

"Thank you, Great White Father, for suicide, TB, alcoholism, despair, poverty, and your other great gifts," said Joe.

"Amen," said Henry.

"Has cynical got a Greek or a Latin root?" said Henry.

"Henry," said Joe, "I really don't give a fuck."

37

"How many of these kids this year?" said Du Pré.

"That makes nine," said Joe, "good little Indians. We'd have more but we have a real good EMT team and an ambulance service that's pretty good."

"You know this kid?" said Du Pré.

"A kid," said Joe, "Danny Bouyer. Father's a drunk and an asshole even when he ain't drunk. Mother's tried, went off, got a associate degree from a business school in Minneapolis, but, you know, there aren't that many businesses here on the res and it's hard to get capital together out of your welfare checks. She played bingo a lot."

"Danny get in trouble?" said Du Pré.

"Shoplifting," said Joe, "Couple candy bars or some such shit. Look, there was something wrong with the kid. Talk to him, and it would take him forever to answer a question. Like his mind kept burping and farting and he couldn't concentrate for ten seconds. I don't think he could read. They graduate 'em anyway. I talked to him a couple times. Busted him and some of his friends for drinking beer, sent them all to rehab, he came back just like he went in. He wasn't playin' with a full deck."

"Sweet kid, though," said Henry, "Wouldn' hurt anybody, you know, he loved animals. Sick cats, he liked to take care of sick cats."

"Brother and sisters?" said Du Pré.

"They're better," said Joe, "The girl's doing well in school and the boy plays basketball and he can draw pretty good. They were quite a pair debating, too. Poor Danny, he had trouble talking, too. Like his tongue wouldn't work or something."

Du Pré nodded.

"Well," he said, "I am going to go and talk to the doctor."

"Watch out for white medicine men," said Henry, "they're very superstitious."

The doctor was moving over toward the well. The firefighters had hooks on poles and they were fishing for what was left of Danny Bouyer that hadn't been dropped in the black body bag yet.

" 'Scuse me," said Du Pré, when he got close to the ambling doctor.

The man stopped and he turned around.

He was very blond, with a long intelligent face and kind eyes. He looked tired.

"Yes, Mr. Du Pré," he said.

"Oh," said Du Pré, "We have met maybe?"

The doctor shook his head. "I've heard you fiddle several times. Marvelous. Wonderful music. My name's Redfield. Bill Redfield. Call me Bill, please."

"I am called Du Pré," said Du Pré, "This Jeanne, she is my Madelaine's cousin. I don't know her before, she is in trouble, we come over, try to help. I am the one find poor Danny."

"I heard," said Redfield, "How did you think of this place?"

"Kids always got a secret place," Du Pré said, "There was no place that Danny's body could hide, Jeanne's. So I thought look here. He did not have a gun."

"I gather that usually suicides are very close to where they live," said Redfield, "I suppose he lived here, at least in his heart."

Du Pré nodded. "He had some tough time, I guess."

"I've been here five years," said Redfield, "I used Government money for medical school, and I can repay that by working seven years here. I like these people."

Du Pré nodded. Them Gros Ventré pretty gentle people. Not like them damn Sioux.

"You got a bunch of kids sick from the mine?" said Du Pré.

Redfield's face transformed. It went from a kindly man's to a man truly angry, coldly angry.

"Damn right," he said. "Any kid grows up drinking water out of the pollution plume from that fucking thing, they have bad damage. Heavy metals. Nerves, liver, eyesight, brain damage. Too often they sniff toluol later. It wipes them out right away. It will get anyone, of course, if they expose themselves to it enough. But these kids, about the third time their brains are wiped. It's over."

"You can prove this?" said Du Pré.

Redfield shook his head.

"Irrefutable proof?" said Redfield, "I haven't got the evidence. Oh, I know what is happening. But the mining company points to the low level of metals in the discharge water. The claim the kids could have got poisoned elsewhere. They trot out paid experts to absolve them. It's too expensive a proposition for the tribe to take up, and, anyway, I expect there's money floating around. Human nature. They comply with the standards set by the State of Montana, which are

40

tougher than the Government's. No flies on them. 'Course the State of Montana has gutted the enforcement arm so no one knows what the pollution readings really are. Have to take the mining company's numbers, which, oddly enough, are always acceptable."

Du Pré nodded.

"Most reservations are poor, Du Pré," said Redfield, "Belknap is prostrate. Nearly dead. There are a few jobs in the mines, the pay is good. There's nothing else except a few Government and Tribal jobs."

Du Pré nodded.

"Will you play any music here?" said Redfield.

Du Pré shrugged.

"Friends of mine own a bar in Malta," said Redfield, "I'd call them if you would like to play. Not much good comes around here."

Du Pré looked at the firefighters, hooking and coughing.

"Maybe," he said.

"You live over by the Wolf Mountains?" said Redfield. "Do you know an old man named Benetsee?"

Du Pré looked at Redfield.

Du Pré nodded.

"Maddening old bastard," said Redfield, "Time to time I will have a patient who is sick for no apparent reason I can find. Run tests, nothing, the patient is dying. About four years ago I had one, a woman, who was just wasting away. All the tests I ran were negative. I was transferring her to Billings the next day, but then Benetsee showed up and he burned sweetgrass and he sang a little. Next morning the patient had gained six pounds and she was walking and down in the cafeteria eating. Eating a lot. She was fine a day later."

Du Pré laughed.

"I have another," said Redfield, "Young woman, only seventeen, dying for no apparent reason. If you should see Benetsee, would you ask him to come?"

Du Pré nodded.

"Thanks," said Redfield. He walked on toward the well.

❖ CHAPTER 7 ❖

Du Pré turned into the rutted track that led to Benetsee's cabin. He bumped over the rutted earth and he parked when his transmission case clunked on something. Not a rock. He hoped.

The cabin's front door was open. A young sheepdog, with one blue and one brown eye, ran out barking and wagging its tail at the same time.

Du Pré remembered Benetsee's old dogs, all dead now, how they had woofed and wheezed and farted when he had come, before they went back to the floor by the stove and sank into old dog dreams.

The air was crisp. It would freeze tonight, probably. The last days of August. Fall in Montana. There was new snow on the peaks of the Wolfs already.

Du Pré stepped up on the ramshackle porch, feeling carefully with his feet. The wood was so rotten he could drop through any time. He looked in. The cabin was empty. The stove was going. Red flames shone through the few panes of isinglass left in the door. The holes covered in aluminum foil. Some of them, anyway.

Du Pré went back out and down and he walked on the path around back.

43

The sweatlodge door was down and there was a little steam coming out at the place where it joined the tent.

Du Pré could hear young Pelon chanting. Then Benetsee's deep raspy old voice break and go from creak to falsetto and back to rust.

Du Pré found the cottonwood stump and he sat on the punky wood and he rolled a cigarette. He smoked. After he finished his cigarette he went back to his car and fished out the gallon jug of screwtop wine, white, bubbly, sweetish, and awful, that he had brought for Benetsee. There were a couple old jam jars sitting in the grass by the stump. Du Pré tossed a few bugs out of them and he went to the little creek and he rinsed them out.

Benetsee and Pelon sang on. The sweatlodge steamed.

Du Pré waited.

Old fucker knows that I am here, Du Pré thought, I am pissed enough to leave, he will come out. Not until then. Old bastard.

Sacred songs, Du Pré thought.

As soon as he thought that Benetsee and Pelon began to sing about how they lived in a yellow submarine.

Du Pré cursed. He stalked over to the lodge and he jerked the door open and he threw the flap over the top of the lodge and he bent down and he looked in.

"Don't fuck with me," he yelled, "You old shit. I bring you wine, I have some questions, I bring you tobacco. You old bastard."

Benetsee and Pelon laughed and laughed.

44

"Holy song," said Benetsee, "Real old one."

"Fuck you," said Du Pré.

He went back and sat on the stump. Benetsee came out on his hands and knees, wearing only a yellowed pair of boxer shorts. Pelon, his apprentice, followed, wearing paisley jockey shorts. The two medicine men wiped themselves dry with towels and they put on their clothes. Benetsee's were ragged and old. Pelon was still a dandy. Everything he wore was pressed and clean. His cowboy boots were shined. Benetsee wore old black hightop sneakers.

Benetsee came to Du Pré, grinning.

"You have wine for me?" he said.

Du Pré broke the seal on the wine. He filled a jelly jar with it and handed it to the old man.

Pelon didn't drink alcohol, but he must have one time because he looked wistfully at the jug for a fleeting moment.

"That Redfield, you call him," said Benetsee, "Tell him I come in two days. Girl will be all right."

Du Pré nodded. He had long since ceased to care how Benetsee knew what he knew. It made his head hurt less.

"Pelon," said Du Pré, "You want a smoke maybe? I am rude, I forget to bring you some pop."

"It is all right," said Pelon, laughing, "I don't like that pop so good any more. Too much whiteman sugar."

Du Pré made him a cigarette, and one for Benetsee.

They smoked.

Benetsee drank glasses of wine, he belched happily.

"Danny Bouyer, him," said Du Pré.

Benetsee nodded, but he didn't say anything.

"People are made a lot sick there, Fort Belknap," said Du Pré.

"Bad water," said Benetsee, "I tell them, you got to move but they don't listen, me."

"Ah," said Du Pré, "This Doctor Redfield he is a good man, yes?"

Benetsee nodded.

"He says that there are a lot of kids like poor Danny Bouyer," said Du Pré, "Comes from drinking bad water. But he can't prove it."

Benetsee nodded.

"So I got people, son of my Madelaine's cousin, dying, what do I do?" said Du Pré.

"You know what to do," said Benetsee, "I been telling you, years, but I don't need to any more. You know what to do."

"Eh?" said Du Pré.

"Take care, your people," said Benetsee, "You one of them half-ass Catholic Métis breeds, Red River breeds, you people all over like clap. So take care of them. Be a warrior."

Du Pré sighed.

"OK," he said, "But it is not like I can just shoot somebody, you know."

"Any fool can shoot somebody," said Benetsee, "It takes a warrior, take care of the people."

"I am making a joke," said Du Pré, feeling foolish.

46

"Me, too," said Benetsee, having more wine.

Pelon laughed.

"Why don't you send, Thunder Bunny here?" said Du Pré, looking at Pelon.

"Him got other things to do," said Benetsee, "I am teaching him. What he is doing, takes brains."

Du Pré laughed.

"OK," he said, "What do I do."

"We are hungry," said Benetsee, "Take us to the bar, we have something to eat, maybe I dance with Madelaine, some."

Du Pré drove to Madelaine's and got her and the four of them went down to the bar.

Bart and Big Jim were there, talking in low voices in the corner about something. They looked up and waved and went back to talking.

Benetsee and Pelon ordered big thick steaks and trimmings. The old man drank more wine. His black eyes gleamed and he giggled from time to time. Pelon drank water.

"Pelon," said Benetsee, "He is a bad drunk once, he keep his job but he is a pretty bad drunk. He piss in one of them computers once. They never figure out he done it."

Du Pré nodded.

Benetsee looked at Madelaine. He took her hand and they went off to the dance floor and two-stepped some. Madelaine was a head taller than the old man.

"Sweetgrass Hills," said Pelon, "them miners, they will

eat them. Chew them up, shit them out, take the gold, don't leave nothing left but bad water and dead rock."

Du Pré nodded.

"Pret' holy place," said Pelon, "I am told when I was a child that when I die, I go to Sweetgrass Hills live there forever."

Flatheads believe that, Du Pré thought, maybe some others. Them Flatheads speak that Salishan tongue. Come over from the coast, not too long ago.

Big Jim might know when.

What about the Sweetgrass Hills?

Heaven.

Benetsee and Madelaine came back and they sat down.

"Jeanne she don't tell us much we are there," said Madelaine.

Du Pré looked at her.

"Before Danny is born she was living with that Gros Ventré bastard on that Kelly Creek," said Madelaine, "But she leave there before she is carrying the other two kids. So they are all right kind of. But Danny he is not, he dies, he is never right."

"She don't want to tell that," said Benetsee, "She think it is her fault. She don't make a mistake, nobody knows."

Madelaine nodded.

"Kid's retarded when he is born. The Gros Ventré bastard beat her up, she is giving him bad children."

Du Pré nodded.

"She is a pret' smart woman," said Madelaine, "But she don't know."

"What is this?" said Du Pré, "Why we can't stop them, huh?"

Benetsee looked at him.

He nodded.

"I don't know what I do about this?" said Du Pré.

Benetsee nodded. He drank some more wine.

✤ CHAPTER 8 ✤

D u Pré and Bassman and Tally were playing flat out. They were on a stage set up at the edge of a park at the Big Sky Ski Resort. A lot of really white people in shorts and hiking boots and polypropylene jackets in vulgar colors were standing and sitting out front clapping and cheering. Some were dancing European peasant dances or passably imitating the clogging of the Gaels. Learned, no doubt, from videos.

There was a TV film crew out there filming them.

Du Pré felt like a fish in a tree. The resort was garish and the houses and condos were ugly in their efforts to be beautiful. Lots of hand-hewn beams and cedar siding.

Out past the crowd foursomes ground around a golf course.

There were many booths selling yuppie beers and small bottlings of California wines from family vineyards once Italian and now owned by dentists and real estate brokers.

Du Pré had seen a sign on a horse barn driving in.

ZEN HORSEMANSHIP CLINIC SEPT. 6–8.

Du-Pré was fiddling a song of the voyageurs to people whose idea of a voyage was to punch buttons on the channel changer and find Tibet.

That Bassman he is listening to lots of that reggae music,

Du Pré thought as he stopped for a break and let the bass player stretch out. Fine with me. Them Métis would like reggae. Us Métis, we like that good music. Don't care what kind but good. Has to be that.

Du Pré came back in and they finished the song and their set and they waited a moment, bowing and smiling, while the crowd made pale noise and whistled.

"Damn," said Bassman, "You see a place like this before. I am up in the shopping places and I see a leather bag sells three thousand dollars. Shit, man, I can make one for fifty. Got plenty old brass hinges and snaps and clips. Three thousand dollars. What is the leather? Off of the Queen of England's dogs?"

"Yeah," said Du Pré, "These ski resorts they got money for sure. Hamburger six bucks. Pretty good burger, but six bucks? You ever do that skiing?"

Bassman shook his head.

They walked to the side of the stage and they cased their instruments.

The young blonde woman who was running the festival came to them and she handed three envelopes out. She got them mixed up but so what?

"Thanks for helping us celebrate diversity," she said. Her teeth were very large and white and straight.

Du Pré nodded. He rolled a cigarette.

"Ugh," she said, "Tobacco. Well, thanks again." She walked off. She had a nice ass.

"I thought we were playin' that good music and here we are celly-brating perversity," said Bassman, grinning, "I

51

guess that means Indians and niggers is allowed here. Don't see any, the golf course."

Du Pré laughed.

"Here is your check, Tally," said Du Pré, handing over the envelope he had been given. Bassman gave Du Pré his, and Tally gave Bassman his.

They opened the envelopes. The checks were in the wrong envelopes.

Du Pré and Tally and Bassman exchanged checks.

"Hey," said Bassman, "They spell my name right like it is French. It is good spelling. Me, I am a stupid Red River Breed, can't spell it that good, me. I wonder, I can get this cashed."

Du Pré's check was made out to Dupree.

"Mine's all right," said Tally.

"Good," said Du Pré, "You buy gas, we get home."

They carried their instruments to Du Pré's old cruiser, sitting in the parking lot with no SUVs parked anywhere near.

"My poor-ass old cruiser it has the clap maybe," said Du Pré, looking at all the expensive four-wheel drive wagons.

"This country they think poor is a disease," said Tally, "We are invited to that party after the last concert. Let's piss them off. Let's go to that party, have fun."

Du Pré snorted.

"Can't smoke there I bet," he said.

"Yah," said Tally, "Prolly not."

"This is not us," said Bassman, "We take this money, go home. I don't got, talk to these silly people. Let's cash these checks, go get a drink, bottle for the road, we go on home. They don't even got dust here. Dust, probably illegal."

"Du Pré! Tally! Bassman!" said a big voice. It was Big Jim Lascaux. He was wearing a half-acre of hat, boots, jeans, and a down vest that was mostly patches.

A police car was following Big Jim, back fifty feet.

Jim walked up, grinning.

"Those cops still on my ass back there?" he said. "They think I am some sort of outlaw dope dealer or something. Been following me all of an hour."

Du Pré nodded.

"Some place here," said Big Jim, "You headed back?"

"We want to cash, these checks," said Du Pré, "Then we maybe head back home. Go to Livingston, maybe. Good hamburgers, Livingston, don't cost six bucks."

"You hear about what happened last Saturday?" said Big Jim.

Du Pré shrugged.

"The ski hill's owned by Boyne Mountain, big ski company from Michigan. They send out some doofus, run the place. He decides to raise the morale of whatever employees he's fucking at the moment, and he has a box of lobsters shipped out, clams, what have you. Charters a helicopter. Flies everybody back into the Spanish Peaks Wilderness Area and sets the chopper down by a lake."

Du Pré laughed.

"Big no-no, since no motorized vehicles are allowed in wilderness. Backcountry ranger pops out from behind every tree and gives them one big ticket. The press has been roasting the doofus ever since. I love these flatlanders."

"Why they want to go to the wilderness in a helicopter?" said Du Pré.

"Indeed," said Big Jim, "Why?"

The cops had stopped ten feet away. There were two of them, young, staring through dark glasses.

Three Indians in worn ranch clothes and a giant in worn ranch clothes. Standing next to a ratty old car that used to be a police car.

The doors opened and the cops got out.

"Evening," said the one on the right.

Du Pré and Tally and Bassman and Big Jim stared at them.

"Come for the festival?" said the other.

Big Jim had taken a small notebook and a felt-tip pen out of his vest pocket. He walked to the first cop and wrote something and then he glanced at the second and wrote something.

"Where you boys from?" said the cop on the right.

"Montana," said Big Jim, "Now would you mind awfully explaining to me just why you are bothering us?"

"We keep a close eye on the place," said the cop on the left.

"Kiss my ass," said Big Jim. Du Pré looked over at him. He was getting mad.

Du Pré stepped in front of the archaeologist.

"We played at the festival," said Du Pré, "Here is one of the checks. He is a friend of ours, got a bad temper. Me, I am a Brand Inspector." He pulled out his badge.

The cops looked at each other, nodded, and they left.

Du Pré clapped Big Jim on the shoulder.

"I got a real bad temper," said Big Jim, "And I don't like pricks. What bastards. You come here and play music for 'em and then they want to roust you."

"It is a rich people's place," said Du Pré.

"Hey, Jim," said Bassman, "We go and cash these checks, buy you a drink. It is all right. They do this, us, a lot. Do it, Billings, do it, Rapid City. Indians, probably bad people. Me, I was pretty bad a long time, spent a lot of time, jail. Drunk. Stole. Got in fights."

"Well," said Big Jim, "I been in jail, too."

"Me, too," said Tally.

Du Pré remembered a couple of times he had spent a night in a room made of steel bars.

"We are badass guys," Du Pré said, "Let's go get this money. Can't even spell our names right, we better."

They went together up to the huge lodge. The folk festival had an office there. The young blonde woman who had given them the misspelled checks was there.

"We need to cash these," said Du Pré.

"The checks are *good*," she said.

Du Pré sighed. "We need the money, get home on," he said.

The young woman made a couple calls and then she took them down a long corridor to an office and a man in a blazer cashed all three checks.

"Thank you," said Du Pré to the young woman. She smiled shallowly and she scurried off.

They went into a bar. They sat on stools.

55

The barman ignored them.

"Let's go to Livingston," said Big Jim, "Fore I break some necks."

They went back out to the parking lot and drove off in Du Pré's cruiser and Big Jim's high-slung four-wheel drive pickup.

They went out to the highway and turned left.

They drove fast down the canyon.

"Hey," said Tally, "This Gallatin River it is all green, got that algae in it some . . . "

High-class shit feed that algae, Du Pré thought, and I know where it come from.

✤ CHAPTER 9 ✤

N ot like them Canadian festivals got real people at them, eh, Du Pré?" said Madelaine. She was laughing.

"Funny place," said Du Pré, "I don't think we play there again."

"Thousand bucks, two days work, not bad," said Madelaine.

Du Pré shrugged.

"Well, they got all this money, got all the save-the-whales stickers the car bumpers," he said, "and the Gallatin River, it runs green with that algae. Sewage and fertilizer, run in the river from that Big Sky. Pret' crazy people. Like them people came here, the wolf crap."

"Silly people," said Madelaine, "I remember them."

"Well," said Du Pré, "They are not here yet and when they come I will maybe just shoot them all."

"That is wrong, Du Pré," said Madelaine, "'Sides they don't come here it is too tough place. Why you think them whites took so long steal this, the Indians maybe? Too tough."

Du Pré laughed.

The telephone rang. Madelaine went to her bedroom and

she picked it up and she just listened. Time to time she would talk, very low.

Du Pré went out back and he looked at the colors on the flanks of the mountains, where the buckbrush had turned and the aspens. The foothills were far off and the dust haze gentled the lines. The mountains were hazy, the light filtered.

Du Pré rolled a smoke and he sat at the picnic table. The breeze had some little cold teeth in it and it was fall. Du Pré smelled it in the air. He remembered the pungent reek of bore cleaner, when at the end of the day he and Catfoot had deer in the garage hanging and they were wiping down the rifles and scrubbing the barrels inside with brass brushes and Hoppe's #9 gunpowder solvent.

Du Pré went back in and Madelaine was still talking. She didn't like to talk on the telephone much and it was a long conversation for her. Du Pré shrugged. He made a cup of coffee and he put a shot of whiskey in it.

He went back out and looked at the mountains and thought of fat mule deer.

"Du Pré!" Madelaine called through the door, "Jeanne is very sick. She is very drunk and she is talking, she kill herself."

Du Pré stood up. He dropped his cigarette on the grass and he ground it out.

"You call that Bart," she said, "We maybe fly, Fort Belknap, you know. She is not well. Her kids, they are scared."

Du Pré nodded.

"I call that Dr. Redfield," said Du Pré, "Then we drive over."

"Fly," said Madelaine.

"Drive," said Du Pré, "Me, I know you, you will bring her kids back here with you. So they will have things they want to bring. Bart's planes, little jets, maybe can't land there anyway."

"OK," said Madelaine, "You call that doctor."

Du Pré did. He waited a few moments while the nurse found Dr. Redfield.

"Jeanne is sick drunk, suicidal," said Du Pré, "We are coming over, maybe take her kids, take her to hospital."

"Oh," said Redfield, "Poor Jeanne. I'll get someone from Alcohol Services right over there. We can detox her here but she may need to go to a treatment center. I don't know if she's been before."

"Don't know either," said Du Pré, "We drive there."

"See you," said Redfield, hanging up.

Madelaine was packing a few things in a bag. Du Pré grabbed some cheese and bread and onions and some potato chips and he got a jug of water and some whiskey in a flask and some extra bags of Bull Durham.

Five minutes later they were blazing down the highway at ninety.

There was little traffic. The deer hunters would not be here for over a month and there wasn't much on the local two-lane blacktop but an occasional rancher in a pickup hauling feed or checking fence.

Du Pré reached back in the car and he found his whiskey and he opened it and he had a drink.

"My drunk goes to help someone who's drunk," said Madelaine.

59

Du Pré shrugged. I drink too much, smoke too much, only thing she don't think I do too much is fuck.

"I fuck too much?" said Du Pré.

Madelaine punched him in the ribs.

"Animal," she said, laughing.

Du Pré drove.

"Poor Jeanne, she have very bad luck," said Madelaine, "She is always unhappy, her aunt say."

"That Redfield he will see her to the hospital," said Du Pré, "I don't know these kids, you do?"

"Teenage kids," said Madelaine, "Probably we want to kill them after ten minutes, but they are just kids."

Madelaine ate snotty teenage badass kids like popcorn, spit out the hulls, make the hulls clean their room, Du Pré thought, she scare the shit out of me, too.

They got to the Indian Health Service hospital in Lodgepole and Du Pré let Madelaine off by the emergency entrance and he went on and parked out of the way. An ambulance came in not two minutes later and the attendants rushed someone on a gurney inside. The person on the gurney had gray hair.

Du Pré went in the main entrance and he asked the nurse for the number of Jeanne's room and he got it and directions and he went down the hall and stopped by the door. The door was almost shut. He tapped lightly on it.

He could hear someone sobbing.

Madelaine whistled low and Du Pré slipped in and he waited by the curtain that separated Jeanne's bed from another which was empty.

Jeanne was babbling and sobbing and Madelaine was holding her hand and stroking her hair.

A nurse came in and she smiled at Du Pré. She had a little paper cup with some pills and a small glass of water.

"I give them to her," said Madelaine.

"I have to see her swallow them," said the nurse, "Hospital rules. But you go ahead and get her to do that and I'll just watch." She was young and bright and she had strong Gros Ventré features, the axblade nose and the height. The Big Bellies were big people. Good strong bones.

Jeanne took the pills and she swallowed some water and she lay back down. Her face was red and swollen and her eyes bleary. She reeked of booze and hopelessness.

"Great," said the nurse. She patted Madelaine's arm and she left, smiling at Du Pré.

Du Pré went outside after a while and he smoked. Madelaine came out before he was done and she was looking sad.

Du Pré put his arm around her.

"Booze take somebody, it is sad," she said. She had lost two uncles she loved to alcohol and a brother to drugs and another brother had died in a car wreck because he was drunk.

"Just eat some people right up," said Madelaine, "Eats up the sad ones. I love that Bart, how he keeps sober, even though it is sad for him and he is lonely. I don't know if poor Jeanne will want to live, not drink. She has been in them hospitals many times."

Du Pré nodded.

"She just went to sleep," said Madelaine, "That Dr. Redfield he come after you are gone and he talk with me and her a little. She is pretty groggy. He said there is an Indian place she can go to, they do sweats and burn that sweet grass, pray."

"We take her kids?" said Du Pré.

"We go talk to them," said Madelaine, "Redfield he say the daughter is already a powerful woman and the boy is a good boy. Maybe they want to stay here be with their friends, they don't know nobody in Toussaint 'cept me a little bit."

They got in Du Pré's old cruiser and they went off to Jeanne's little modular house. There was a boy of twelve or so sitting on the front step. He stood up when Du Pré and Madelaine got out of the car.

He came to them and he was smiling.

"I am Jimmy," he said, "you are that Madelaine and that Du Pré?" He had on a black sweatshirt with the logo of a rock band Du Pré had never heard of and jeans and running shoes. He was very clean.

"Uh," said Madelaine, "Where is that Mickey?"

"She is inside, cooking," said Jimmy. "Come on."

He led them into the house.

The washing machine and dryer were going and the place smelled of soap and hot electrical appliances.

Mickey was in the kitchen frying meat brown. She was a small woman, a girl, fourteen or fifteen, with a pretty face and her head was swathed in a towel. She motioned Du Pré and Madelaine to chairs.

She waved her hands by her face and moved her fingers in sign language.

"You sign?" said Jimmy.

Madelaine and Du Pré shook their heads.

"Mickey, she cannot hear or speak," said Jimmy, "But she read lips and she sign good. She can yell, those fingers." He laughed and she hugged him and then they both smiled.

Madelaine clapped her hands together and she laughed.

"Well," she said, "What you kids want to do 'bout this?"

❖ CHAPTER 10 ❖

Well, I would have been a little worried, you going to Zortman," said Dr. Redfield, "But I don't any more."

Big Jim Lascaux was sitting with Du Pré and the doctor in a saloon in Malta.

"Who is this guy," said Redfield, "who's flying Jeanne to Wisconsin?"

"Bart Fascelli," said Du Pré, "He is a good man. Bad time with booze, he has much money which he tries to handle well. Good friend. Madelaine ask him, he fly Jeanne to the moon."

"One of the Chicago and Detroit Fascellis?" said Redfield.

"Yah," said Du Pré.

"I see," said the doctor.

"Bart's been helping me do my research for years," said Big Jim, "But the one thing he demanded was I not tell anyone who was writing the big checks. I'll say he's a good friend. I was in a wreck, busted up pretty bad after my divorce, owed everybody, and I think when they are letting me out of the hospital on crutches how the fuck am I gonna pay for all of this. Haven't seen anyone about that. So I ask and they say I have had my bill paid. Lawyer says the same thing. Wife's paid off. I have money in the bank I don't know I have. Money paid

64

the IRS I owe on all this. I never asked Bart, of course, but it couldn't be anyone else."

"Hmm," said Redfield.

"Them kids will be fine," said Du Pré, "That little Mickey she is some woman, eh?"

Redfield laughed. "Oh, yes," he said. "Can't hear and can't speak but she gets on well. Jeanne has other people here, they'll look in on Mickey and Jimmy. They'll be fine."

"Uh," said Du Pré, "Mickey, she was born like that?"

Redfield nodded.

"She . . . Jeanne drinking that bad water when Mickey . . . ?" said Du Pré.

"Maybe," said Redfield, "But thing is that the heavy metals stay on. It takes a long time for them to leach out of a human body. Mickey could have been affected, or it could have been something else."

Du Pré looked at him.

"I'm a doctor," said Redfield, "I have to be absolutely sure. Morally, I'm certain it was the water. Scientifically, I cannot say for sure."

"How'd you end up in the Indian Health?" said Big Jim.

"Poor boy," said Redfield, "so I traded seven years of my professional life for a professional life."

"Where you from?"

"Northern Michigan," said Redfield, "Both my parents were alcoholics and both died of it. I wanted out of jackpine Michigan, and I made it. But I like it here. I could make more money in private practice, of course, but I don't care about money. Just so I have enough."

Big Jim nodded.

"Du Pré tell you about the Sweetgrass Hills?" said Big Jim.

"No," said the doctor, "But Persephone utterly destroys whatever they mine, and much else. Gold. Gold. Gold."

"I suspect that may be one of the great archaeological sites in North America," said Big Jim, "Maybe the most important for the early stuff. I hate to see it ruined."

"Well," said Redfield, "I wouldn't speak about that in Zortman. The miners are happy to have those well-paying jobs."

Du Pré nodded. People, they got to eat, want to raise their families. Live. Need those jobs.

Redfield finished his drink and he got up. He had sipped just one while Big Jim and Du Pré had had, like good Montana boys, six. Each.

"You guys," said Redfield, "I can't do liver transplants. All you Montanans either drink like fools or you had to quit."

He smiled and he walked out.

"I believe I just heard a discouraging word," said Big Jim.

"He is a good guy," said Du Pré, "But people like him they don't do nothing bad for them. They might enjoy it."

Big Jim laughed.

"We'll go and see old Piney and after that we can try out Zortman," said Big Jim. "You know what hurts me worst about all this?"

Du Pré looked at him.

"If we can save the Sweetgrass Hills," said Big Jim, "We're gonna have to suck up to those little assholes were at your performance in Big Sky. Days I think rather than leave

Montana to 'em I'd just as soon see the whole place dug up and burned. Shoot the fucking eagles. So what?"

"This fine country," said Du Pré, "It will survive even them."

They got up and went out to Big Jim's black four-wheel pickup. The windows were tinted very dark. He didn't get stopped much. The back bumper had one sticker on it.

I JUST GOT OUT OF DEER LODGE FOR KILLING A NOSY SON OF A BITCH.

Big Jim wheeled the rig out of the saloon parking lot and he headed out of town south. They came to a sign for veterinary services and Big Jim turned and he parked by a low building that stretched out behind to a series of chutes and corrals.

They got out and went in. A gray-haired man with a very long jaw and fierce blue eyes was standing by the front counter. He was yelling into the phone.

"Myrtle, god damn it," he roared, "I keep tellin' ya I have never seen the skeleton of a cat up in a tree. Fluffy will come down . . . yeah. I know the fire department won't help. You call them every time that fat son of a bitch crawls up there. . . . Myrtle, quit yelling. I like Fluffy, OK . . . have a drink. OK OK. Bye, Myrt."

He hung up. He turned and looked at Big Jim and Du Pré.

"You Lascaux?" he said.

Jim nodded.

"This that fiddlin' son of a bitch of a Red River Breed?"

Du Pré nodded.

"Damn," said the vet, "My life's just brimful of pleasures. Now, I hear you are wonderin' about what these damn heap-leach mines do to people? Well, bad things."

"Like what?" said Du Pré, "I talk to the doctor, Redfield, and he say he can't prove nothin'."

"Probably can't," said the vet.

"Why he tell us to come see you?" said Du Pré.

"Because," said the vet, "I can damn well prove what that polluted water does to animals."

"Ah," said Big Jim.

"Call me Piney," said the vet, "everybody pretty well has all my damn life."

Du Pré and Big Jim nodded.

"Well," Piney roared, "Let's go get a goddamned drink and then we'll go take a look at some of my exhibits. You'll need the drink. Exhibits aren't very pretty."

The telephone rang.

Piney glared at the telephone. He waited until Myrtle's voice came out of the answering machine and then he stalked out the front door. He didn't bother locking it.

They drove back down to the saloon and went in.

Piney waved to the woman behind the bar and he joshed with a couple ranchers sitting having red beers. There was a man in a red mackinaw at the far end of the bar, big and bald, drinking a big tall highball.

Piney tapped him on the shoulder.

When the man turned Piney hit him hard on the jaw, knocking the man off the stool and down to the floor. Piney kicked him for a while until the man was still.

"I told that son of a bitch to get out of my country," said Piney, "Lying bastard anyway."

"Uh, Piney," said the woman behind the bar, "That's . . . not Norris. That's some guy I never seen before sort of looks like Norris . . . "

"What the hell do you mean it ain't Norris?" said Piney.

"It isn't Norris," said the woman.

Piney turned the guy over and he looked a long time at the man's face.

"You're right," said Piney, "It isn't Norris."

"Well," said the woman behind the bar, "I told you it wasn't Norris."

"Why," said Piney, "didn't you tell me that it wasn't Norris before I hit him?"

"Since it wasn't Norris I didn't expect you to hit him," said the woman behind the bar.

The guy on the floor groaned and moved a little.

"New glasses," said Piney, "I could have sworn it was Norris."

Big Jim and Du Pré were looking at each other and trying very hard not to laugh hysterically.

"Piney is something of a warmonger," said Big Jim.

"Uh," said Du Pré.

"Piney," said the woman behind the bar, "What are you going to do about all of this?"

"I'll sue you," said Piney, "For falsely allowing someone who looks enough like Norris to sit at Norris's place at your bar and gull me into hitting them."

Piney stomped out of the bar, cursing.

The guy on the floor sat up.

"Piney's mellowed," said the woman behind the bar, "Couple years ago even he woulda bit the guy's ear off."

"Come on," said Big Jim to Du Pré, "Let's go see what Piney's got."

✦ CHAPTER 11 ✦

T hat was about enough to make me puke," said Big Jim, "What got me the worst was those ducklings."

One of Piney's exhibits was a jar filled with formalin and hatchlings. The ducks had been born without the tops of their skulls, or beaks.

They were back in the Sweetgrass Hills, up on the top of a ridge which hunkered over the archaeological dig. It was late afternoon and the cheatgrass and jackgrass was pale red and metallic in the sinking light.

What got me the worst was them firemen fishing little Danny Bouyer out of the old well piece by piece, Du Pré thought, and you never forget that smell. Nothing else smells like that.

"He's got all those aborted calves," said Big Jim, "and the deformed lambs, the wild animals. Even the damned chickens. Pretty good evidence. You hear about what heavy metals do. Seeing it is something else."

Du Pré stared down at the land. He could see the faint traces of the shoreline of a lake that once had covered a hundred acres or so, now filled in and then the lake bottom became a meadow and the water cutting down through the stone under the soil had dropped the stream channel and then more little streams reached out like the veins from the stem of a leaf. But once this had been a big lake and animals had come to water here and the hunters had waited for them and if there was meat in the camp the people would have full bellies and they would dance and sing. They would have been happy.

Not so long ago, Du Pré thought.

"We found an old bog that these people drove the mammoths into so they'd be slowed by the mud and they killed them there," said Big Jim, "The water table dropped so the bog is a foot under the soil. Full of bones and stone tools and we can tell from the pollen which century it was. We can go back thirteen thousand years now and we still have eight feet of deposits to bedrock," said Big Jim.

"Who these people were?" said Du Pré.

"We don't know," said Big Jim, "So long ago. Could be the ancestors of the Shoshones. But we just don't know."

Sioux move west, 1700s, Crows move west, the Sioux push them, Crows shove the Shoshones south, Shoshones shove the Utes south . . . Du Pré thought I don't think many tribes spent very long, one place. Two hundred years ago, them Cheyennes raising pumpkins, corn in Iowa. Us Métias, we marry anybody, go where they go. Good Catholic people, make a lot of children.

"Hey," said Big Jim, "Look over there." He was pointing across the old playa lake to a man walking on a path cattle had cut into the side hill.

"He didn't come in by the road," said Big Jim, "If he . . . coming that way he's twenty miles from the highway."

Du Pré squinted and stared. He watched the man move.

"That's Pelon," said Du Pré.

"Oh," said Big Jim.

"He is that young guy, lives at Benetsee's," said Du Pré, "Good guy. Benetsee is getting old, probably gone to die soon. Making sure there is someone, give me shit all my days."

"The shaman," said Big Jim.

"He is an old son of a bitch," said Du Pré, "Riddle Man."

Big Jim lit a cigarette.

"They pretty much are," he said, "All the ones I know are, anyway."

"You know Benetsee?" said Du Pré.

"Heard of him," said Big Jim.

"Well," said Du Pré, "This Pelon he is studying, be as big a prick as that Benetsee. But I had better go, talk to him. He don't walk there, so I see him, he don't want to talk to me."

"Go right up on the ridge," said Big Jim, "There's a trail heads north just the other side. You walk quick, you'll meet him in the next lakebed over."

Du Pré nodded. He started off up the path and he went to the top and he stepped over the plates of rock that stuck up like a spine of a buried monster on the ridgeline. The path was ten feet on, a wide one that was worn very deep into the earth.

Buffalo trail. Them buffalo, too, they never go anywhere unless they got a reason.

Du Pré walked on, picking his footing carefully. There were little piles of rock flakes and larger stones and the trail zigzagged.

Them buffalo, they look out of one eye, walk that way,

73

look out of the other one, walk that way a while. Eyes on opposite sides of their head. Pret' easy, spot a buffalo trail. It don't look like nothin' else.

The trail was descending, gently. Du Pré had easy walking. He got to the edge of the old lake bed and at that moment Pelon stepped out of the narrow little arroyo that led through the hills from one playa to the other.

Du Pré waved. Pelon waved back but he kept walking.

They met in the middle of the meadow.

"Eh, Pelon," said Du Pré, "What that old bastard have you tell me?"

"He say you come see him when you get back," said Pelon, "Sweat with him. For the spirit of Danny Bouyer."

Du Pré nodded.

Pelon grinned at Du Pré.

Du Pré shrugged and he rolled them both a smoke. He lit one with his shepherd's lighter and he handed it to Pelon and then he lit one for himself.

"Good tobacco," said Pelon, "I like that Bull Durham."

"Pret' good," said Du Pré.

They smoked.

"Benetsee, he tell me come here and fast and pray," said Pelon, "So I will be here a while. I ask him where, he say I will know it I see it."

Du Pré nodded. Benetsee's directions were like that.

"I can only drink a little water," said Pelon, laughing. "Me, I don't like to fast. I like, cheeseburgers."

Du Pré took out a little jerky from his shirt pocket and he offered it to Pelon, who shook his head.

"You come back here maybe a week, ten days," said Pelon, "You check around, maybe I am dead. Starved to death. Feeding the coyotes."

"OK," said Du Pré.

"Probably not," said Pelon, "That Benetsee he have no one, play jokes on, I die."

"He got me," said Du Pré.

"He say you hardly any fun anymore," said Pelon, "Him say he go away for a while and you start asking the sky."

Du Pré shrugged.

"He is worried," said Pelon.

Du Pré looked at him.

"He tell you what?" said Du Pré finally.

Pelon shook his head.

"I am following the hunters," said Pelon, "They come from over there west and they come through there. Used to be two lakes here, big ones, lots of birds, good water. Long time ago."

Du Pré nodded.

"They come down the Great North Trail," said Pelon, "They come down here and they eat them mammoths, they eat that big sloth. Big fucker, that sloth. They walk across from Siberia and they come down here, long time."

Du Pré waited.

"They come right through here," said Pelon.

Du Pré nodded.

"Me, I can hear them," said Pelon.

Du Pré smiled.

"Week, ten days, come see me," said Pelon, "I follow

them. Long time though them hunters, they don't need to eat. Maybe I starve to fucking death."

Du Pré nodded.

"I am happier with my computers sometime I think," said Pelon, "But I guess not. Pretty strange out here. I got one blanket, it will be cold tonight."

It will frost tonight, Du Pré thought. "You, freeze your ass."

"I will go," said Pelon, "Thanks for the tobacco."

Du Pré watched him go. He smiled. He went back down the trail that Pelon had come up. He closed his eyes to slits so the world was gray and out of focus, and he could see only the larger shapes of the hills.

Lake sure sticks out like this, Du Pré thought, I bet the other lake is higher and there was a spring over there, good water, don't got a lot of animal shit in it. Over north there is a mile of ice sticking up in the air and melting, the Missouri is a hundred times the size it is now. Glaciers over west, sliding down out of the mountains, over east, sliding down out of Canada.

Winds must have been real strong. That would be a good place to camp out of the wind, it go by overhead.

Camp here.

More water, so there is more trees for firewood.

Wonder if they had to make war, keep this place?

Don't you always have, make war, keep a place?

He walked on.

❧ CHAPTER 12 ❧

D r. Stone tapped his hammer on a big boulder of reddish rock. The rock rang a little.

"That," he said, "Is a chunk of Canada. The ice brought it down. Out east the ice brought down cubic miles of rock and gravel. It brought diamonds to Indiana. Diamonds occur only in pipes that come straight up from deep in the earth. No one knows where the Canadian pipes are. Probably under a lake. A quarter of Canada is under lakes."

Du Pré looked at the boulder. It weighed several tons.

"Tongues of ice sliding under their own weight," said Stone, "When ice gets to be fifty meters thick it begins to move downhill. It liquefies and slides. The ice in Canada may have been two miles high. There was so much ice in the Northern Hemisphere that the oceans were three hundred feet lower than the oceans are today."

They were standing on the High Plains west of the Sweetgrass Hills. An arch of clouds hung over the distant Rocky Mountain Front, hidden by the curve of the earth. The mountains were hidden but the weather above them was not.

"How come them Sweetgrass Hills never had ice on them?" said Du Pré.

Stone shrugged.

"Ice flows went on either side of them," he said, "and held off other ice flows. The way a low island in a river may be spared if the currents force water away from it. There are plants in the Sweetgrass Hills that don't belong there if the ice covered everything and then the plants had to recolonize. Rainfall changed. The Great Plains were forested ten thousand years ago. The rain diminished and the grass slowly took over."

"They come down from Red River," said Du Pré, "come through here, long time, more than a century ago. Red River carts. Wheels made of rounds cut from cottonwoods. Held together with rawhide. Didn't have metal. Build corrals, drive them buffalo in, kill them, make meat for the winter, pemmican, fill the parfleches. Fight off them Sioux, them Blackfeet. Dance. Play cards. Sing. Fight. Get meat and go back home."

"This gold," said Du Pré, "How does it come here?"

"A lowgrade ore," said Stone, "Very low. Until the price of gold got very high and the technology sophisticated this ore wouldn't pay to mine. Now, practically any traces of gold can be concentrated and got out. Bash the rock up and trickle cyanide solution over the pile, gather the enriched solution in a settling pond and extract the gold. Also, extract the lead and the cadmium and the selenium and whatever."

"Selenium?"

"Very poisonous metal," said Stone, "There's a lot of volcanic ash all over the west that has selenium in it. Woody asters need it to bloom. They find selenium and bring it up. Stock eats it and people eat the meat. People live a long time, they concentrate the selenium. It turns their hearts into great flabby gobs of weak muscle. Lead damages the nervous system and the brain, and especially so in fetuses and young children. Cadmium, too. It isn't nuclear war which will get the human race, Du Pré, it's heavy metals."

"Why they don't take them out when they take out the gold?" said Du Pré.

"Money," said Stone, "It cuts profits to do that. Look, you remember all the uproar about the strip mining of coal? Well, it takes two hundred men a year to mine a million tons of coal from a deep mine, shafts and lifts and the like. It takes ten men to mine a million tons of coal in a year from a strip mine. Miners are well paid. The wages for one hundred and ninety men for a year plus benefits, well, fifteen to twenty million dollars. The coal companies would just as soon keep that money."

Du Pré nodded.

"Let's get back," said Stone. They walked over to a tiny airplane, a Rutan, which had the propellor at the rear of the fuselage and two tiny twin booms to hold the tail assembly. Two seats. Big tires. Du Pré crawled in the one in the back when Stone lifted up the hinged Plexiglas bubble that covered the cockpit and single passenger seat. Stone got in the pilot's spot and he let the bubble down. He and Du Pré fixed the latches. The little plane took off in a few hundred feet, bouncing once and then taking slowly to the air.

Stone flew low, back to the site of the dig in the Sweetgrass Hills. He set down on a dirt runway which had most of the rocks picked out of it.

Stone sat while Du Pré got out and he nodded and goosed the engine a little and he fiddled with the latches and he took off, headed around in a climbing turn, and went south toward Bozeman.

"That damn thing ain't bigger than most parachutes," said Bart.

Du Pré didn't mind anything but the way the wings bent up when the plane took off and all the weight was loaded on the light graphite and glass composite they were made of. They bent a lot.

"Well," said Bart, "I have been trying to charm Piney but it's uphill work. He said I was nothing but a fucking flatlander. Rich flatlander at that. He kept looking at my ear like he wanted to eat it. I dunno, the guy's what? Seventy? Still biting off ears in fights in saloons? I love Montana. I could never bite off someone's ear in a fight. I won't ever belong here, Du Pré."

Du Pré grinned. "Me," he said, "I never bite off no one's ear, a fight. Can't see me do that."

"I can see you biting off someone's ear," said Bart, "It's a quality you guys all have. I can tell it's a Montanan if I know the guy would bite off my ear if we fought."

Piney was off waving his arms at the archaeologist who was running the dig. The archaeologist was laughing.

"Well," said Du Pré, "He . . . uh . . . loves animals."

"Sure," said Bart, "But he eats them."

Piney left off entertaining the archaeologist, who he had called a fucking academic, and he was walking back to Du Pré and Bart.

Du Pré glanced at the Band-Aids on the knuckles of Piney's left hand.

"You are left-handed?" said Du Pré, when Piney got to them.

"Naw," said Piney, "But my left hook's not so good since I had the cataract operation. Messed up my aim. Sumbitchin' eye doctor fucked it up. I got to go talk to him about it sometime."

"Oh," said Bart.

"Yeah," said Piney, "I was aimin' for the guy's nose but I hit his teeth. Came away with three of them in my hand. Weren't false teeth neither. Hurt like a bastard."

"God," said Bart.

"Son," said Piney, "If you believe everything Montanans tell ya you'll be in some sorry trouble. I got bit by a goddamn dog. Knew the dog, too. Well, I wouldn't like a thermometer rammed up my ass neither. I couldn't really blame him. My dog, too. Ungrateful bastard."

"How many dogs you got?" said Du Pré.

"Twenty-seven," said Piney, "What with the kids all grown and gone the wife was lonely . . . "

"Balls," said Bart, "You take every dog of good character folks ask you to put down because they don't want the dog anymore."

"He's slanderin' me," said Piney.

"OK," said Bart, "I'm a flatlander, a rich asshole, worth-

81

less as rat shit on a pump handle, now how do I get to be allowed to put up the money to do the lab work on all these aborted calves and all? How do I make it all right with you?"

"He's showin' promise," said Piney to Du Pré, "He's fightin' back. I always did admire that in a goddamn flatlander, you see it so seldom. I spent *years* collecting that shit. *Years.* How do I know you don't *own* Persephone?"

"I don't own Persephone Mining," said Bart.

"What's the Glenfield Corporation?" said Piney.

"One of my family companies," said Bart, "Why?"

"Well," said Piney, "Your fucking Glenfield Corporation owns seventeen percent of the common stock of Persephone Mining."

"Oh, God," said Bart.

"You didn't know that," said Piney. It was not a question.

"No," said Bart.

"You have so fucking much money you don't know where it is, do you?" said Piney.

Bart shook his head miserably.

"OK," said Piney, "Now that I've hurt your feelings, you can do something nice. You can pay to have my little collection analyzed."

"I'll sell the stock," said Bart.

"Fuck you will," said Piney, "As a major stockholder you'll find out what those swine are up to and we need the information. Don't be a damn fool. We can cut their damned throats and they won't know it's been done till they look sideways and their heads fall off."

"Yeah," said Bart, "I see that."

"Money's like water," said Piney, "It just goes where it needs to."

"OK," said Bart, "We can contract with an independent laboratory."

"Naw," said Piney, "We contract with three of them."

Bart nodded.

"I used to come out here a long time ago before these fucking motorcycle pricks tore it up," said Piney, "Long time ago. With my dad and my granddad. Hunt a few birds, kill an antelope. I love these hills. They got something about them."

Du Pré smiled.

"And Persephone can't have them," said Piney, "I just won't allow it."

❖ CHAPTER 13 ❖

W e talk to Mama every night," said Jimmy Bouyer, "She is pret' happy where she is, thinks she can maybe be well this time."

Du Pré and Madelaine and Jimmy and Mickey were sitting in a little restaurant in Lodgepole and eating cheeseburgers. Jimmy and Mickey had big thick chocolate milk shakes. Du Pré and Madelaine had sodas.

"She really like one counselor," said Jimmy, "Indian woman, they talk a lot."

Mickey smiled and twinkled. She waved her hands and moved her fingers and Jimmy looked at her intently.

"Mickey says she knows everything will be all right," said Jimmy, "She talk to the old people, they say so."

"Old people?" said Madelaine.

"Grandfathers, grandmothers," said Jimmy, looking puzzled, "You know."

Madelaine nodded. Dead people. Ghosts.

Good ghosts though. Part of this earth.

"So," said Madelaine, "You kids are all right? You need anything? You got food, you got a little money?"

Mickey waved her hands.

"Somebody just leave us a couple hundred bucks," said

Jimmy, "So we are fine. Jeanne, she will be back in a couple of weeks. We don't need too much. Don't do drugs, don't drink." He laughed.

Du Pré wondered who had left the money. Bart. Or maybe Redfield. Or maybe some other kind and decent person.

"I wish Danny he was here," said Jimmy, "He was a good guy, till a couple years ago. Good guy. Something happen."

Du Pré looked at the kid.

Mickey touched Jimmy's arm and she got up and smiled at Du Pré and Madelaine. She waved her hands.

"We got to go," said Jimmy, "We thank you. I will tell Jeanne when she call that you were here."

They went out quickly.

Du Pré looked at Madelaine.

"Well?" he said.

"I just want to check, see that they are all right," said Madelaine, "That Mickey, she keeps that house very clean and she is a good one, so young. We go back now I guess."

They drove east for a while and stopped at a roadhouse and they got some drinks and then some drinks to go and they went on. Du Pré drove at eighty or eighty-five. It didn't take that long to get back to Toussaint.

Du Pré parked in front of the bar and they got out and stretched and yawned.

"It is the night for the prime rib," said Du Pré.

"Ah," said Madelaine, "Good. Maybe I eat a good piece of that prime rib and I want to dance some later."

Du Pré did not feel like dancing.

But he nodded. They went in.

Bart and Big Jim were having prime rib and talking intently over in the corner. They didn't look up.

Du Pré and Madelaine sat on stools and when Susan Klein saw them she jerked her head toward the kitchen. Du Pré nodded and Susan brought silverware and napkins when she came down the bar. The place was busy and she was alone.

"You need some help, yes?" said Madelaine.

"If you wouldn't mind," said Susan," I damn well never know whether to have an extra person or not, sometimes everybody comes at once and then it all goes to hell."

Madelaine went off and got an apron and she began to bus the dishes off tables and clean them and carry soiled things back to the kitchen and she and Susan ignored Du Pré so he finally went behind the bar and mixed himself a drink and went on over to Bart and Big Jim.

"I got him up to two hundred thousand," said Big Jim, "I keep to the cheap shots and he ups the ante by ten grand each time. You know, the starving little archaeologist on the very brink of a great discovery whose emaciated corpse is found almost through the last inch of stone around King Tut's tomb."

"I hope," said Bart, "That you don't plan to find King Tut's tomb in the middle of goddamn Montana."

"Make it a million and you got it," said Big Jim, "I have a doctorate. Trust me."

"That," said Bart, "is about right."

"I recall a story about some Texas oilman who paid three million for one of three copies of Caesar's *Gallic Wars*," said Big Jim, "in the original blue ballpoint pen and ink."

"Fuck you," said Bart, "I wouldn't pay more'n two for that."

"Um," said Du Pré, "OK, so you are going to find Tut's tomb, there. He was the one with the gold and one nut or something?"

"Huh?" said Bart.

"OK," said Du Pré, "I am thinking I will go back over to Belknap tomorrow, I want to look around there some."

Bart's face went from laughing to dead serious.

"What you got?" he said.

Du Pré shrugged.

Big Jim pulled a chair over for Du Pré.

"It is maybe nothing," said Du Pré, "We are talking, Jimmy and little Mickey Bouyer. Jimmy, he say that Danny was OK till a couple years ago. How? I . . . me, I thought I would go and look."

Big Jim looked at Du Pré.

"I thought he had always had trouble," said Du Pré, "If he did not always, then I want to know what happened."

"The creek water?" said Bart.

"Me," said Du Pré, "I thought he was fucked up, day one. If he was not, what happened?"

Big Jim nodded.

"That crazy Piney he will give you his stuff," said Du Pré, "Then what about these kids we hear about? The kids grew up drinking that bad water. Danny, did he grow up drinking that bad water?"

Bart looked down at his glass.

He nodded.

"I talk to that Redfield. He has been there for five years, I think," said Du Pré.

"Who else?" said Bart.

"State is supposed to monitor the discharges," said Big Jim, "They'd have records, but they are hard to get at. The mining companies don't like violations to be a matter of public record."

"Well," said Bart, "I didn't like my drunk driving convictions being a matter of public record, but they *are*."

"There is something here that does not make sense," said Du Pré.

"Also," said Du Pré, "I do not know anything about this mining. I mean, what it *does*. That Dr. Stone does, but the Persephone people, they have to know he is against them."

"Oh," said Bart.

"So," said Du Pré.

"OK," said Bart, "I'll find a guy for us."

"To look over the mining operation," said Big Jim.

"Have to be somebody that they do not know," said Du Pré.

"I'll talk to Lawyer Foote," said Bart.

"I am not sure where Jeanne live, she was pregnant with Danny and then with Mickey," said Du Pré. "Also, does this heavy metal stuff make kids deaf and dumb?"

"This," said Bart, "Is one very large onion."

"They don't let you on that land they got, see about any old sites, either?" said Du Pré to Big Jim.

"That mine's been going a long time," said Big Jim, "Back before it got fashionable to look for those things."

"Hey, Du Pré," said Madelaine, passing by, "Your damn prime rib it is up on the bar there for you."

Du Pré got up.

"I be back in three, four days," he said.

Bart nodded.

"Good luck," said Big Jim.

Du Pré went back to where he had been sitting.

He ate the big piece of rare prime meat. He has some more whiskey and a big glass of water for all the salt he dumped on the beef.

He rolled a smoke and sat there watching Susan and Madelaine feed thirty people who changed into another thirty people every forty-five minutes.

Little Mickey, thought Du Pré, she is so cheerful, all locked away there can't hear nothin', has never spoke one word. She is OK. Jimmy is a nice kid, seems bright enough. Big sad place in him.

Mama Jeanne, she is ill but she be back soon.

It is some puzzle, I don't know which goes where.

Maybe go see that damn Benetsee before I go on over. Ask him about poor Pelon. That bastard Benetsee, he think it is a big joke starve the poor guy half to death. Perverse old bastard.

Benetsee.

Take him some wine, tobacco.

Madelaine was taking a break. She came and sat with Du Pré.

"I think I maybe see that Benetsee," said Du Pré, "Then I maybe go back over, Belknap, look around."

"Sure, Du Pré," said Madelaine, "I been watching you thinkin' that this last hour, maybe."

"How you know what I think?"

Madelaine looked at Du Pré.

"Du Pré," she said, "I am your woman, I love you. I always know what you think. You got no walls, got no covers. I read you real good."

"This OK," said Du Pré, "I mean, I go?"

Madelaine sighed, she grinned.

"Another half hour," she said, "I fucking tell you to go. But you are not so slow. You are about right."

"OK," said Du Pré.

"Men," said Madelaine, "Christ."

❖ CHAPTER 14 ❖

There is a Métias in camp, Joe," said Henry. He had his cowboy boots up on his desk and a cigarette dangling unlit from his mouth. "Probably a spy. The Seventh Cavalry is probably behind that butte over there. I forget. Do we burn him at the stake or skin him alive?"

Joe was walking a filthy longhaired blond man back toward the cells. The man struggled and said things in German.

Du Pré shrugged. He had done his Army service in Germany but that had been over thirty years ago now.

"Give him a cup of coffee," said Joe, pausing, "It'll hurt more'n them two things you were thinkin' on. Also, we'd have to cut the firewood. And the last guy we skinned, he wriggled a lot and got blood on my Ralph Lauren chamois shirt."

"You take anything in it?" said Henry.

"Black," said Du Pré.

The German began to scream angrily.

"Ol' Lothar there, he keeps bugging some of our medicine people. Says he wants to take them to Germany and have them lecture good Germans who wish they were good

Indians. I thought when he got deported that last time they wouldn't let him back in."

Du Pré nodded. There was a small but steady stream of loons who wanted to be Indians through all the reservations. What they wanted to be was anyone other than who they were. Du Pré couldn't blame them for that.

A cell door slammed and Lothar began to scream.

Joe came back out, whistling.

"Well," said Henry, handing Du Pré a cup of coffee, "you didn't come here to watch our wonderful team comedy act."

"We want to go on the road," said Joe.

"Lots of pussy and cocaine and gold chains," said Henry.

"The good life," said Joe, "whiteman life."

"This Danny Bouyer," said Du Pré, "I am talking to his little brother. Jimmy, he say Danny was OK till couple of years ago."

"Yeah," said Joe, "He was. We cops, you know, we don't see people so much who are doing well. We see them when they aren't. Danny . . . we popped him for a lid of grass once, he was maybe thirteen?"

"Which happens a lot," said Henry, "These kids are depressed. Not much on the res for them. They look at their parents, parents' friends, then they get sad. Nothing much here. A few make it out but not many."

"I don't know Danny was a good kid," said Joe, "Just not a kid we had to mess with all that much."

"He have friends you have to mess with a lot?" said Du Pré.

Henry and Joe looked at each other.

"Well, one," said Henry, "Billy Grouard. Métias name, mostly Indian though. You damn Métias, you fuck your way everywhere. Anyway, there's a bunch of kids, Billy leads them. We know he leads them, they have secret forts and a gang and all that. We know it's Billy, because he's the only one who's smart enough not to get caught."

"Good basketball player, too," said Joe.

"Good student," said Henry.

"See," said Joe, "These kids, they do things like wear their hair in what they think is a traditional Big Belly warrior style. Big Belly warriors used muskrat grease for their hair, these kids use mousse. So what? They get beer or wine when they can get someone older to buy it for them, and we got more drugs on the res than fucking Sunset Boulevard, of course, and they're like any of the other kids aren't hot for Jesus and flogging their knees night and day, they get stoned and they get drunk and they'd like to screw more."

"I'd like to get drunk and screw more," said Henry.

"Just don't drive and wear a condom, for Chrissakes," said Joe, "Wear a condom over your head."

"Where is this Billy Grouard?" said Du Pré.

"Right now?" said Joe, "He's in school. School lets out, lemme see, about four. Quarter to, something like that."

"I like to talk to him," said Du Pré.

"Yeah," said Henry, "Just remember, when he act stupid he is not. He is smarter than me and Joe. Probably smarter than you."

Du Pré left and he drove slowly over to the high school.

It was a one-story building, spread out. There were some old cars in the parking lot. Litter.

Du Pré looked at it.

This place makes me sad, he thought, I am in it long ago, it bores me some.

He got out and walked up the sidewalk to the front door and he went on in the foyer. Cases of trophies. Some paintings by students. A list of athletic events. The place smelled of floorwax and disinfectant.

Du Pré saw an open door. There was a sound of typing coming out of it. He went to the door and looked in. Two Indian women were sitting at desks, looking at piles of papers. Typing.

Du Pré knocked on the door jamb. They looked up.

"May we help you?" said one.

"I am looking for Billy Grouard," said Du Pré, "I am a friend of his people."

The women looked at each other.

"He will be out of last class, five minutes," said the woman who had spoken before, "He pass out that hall there. To his old car."

"What kind of car?"

The woman got up and she walked to Du Pré and motioned toward the front door. They walked to it.

She scanned the lot a moment.

"That old red car got the plastic on the window," she said, pointing.

Du Pré thanked her and he went out and he sat on the hood of his old cruiser and he rolled a smoke and he waited.

94

A bell rattled.

In a minute kids began to spill out the door, laughing, yelling, or walking quietly with their books in their arms.

Du Pré saw a tall, very good-looking kid with roached hair come out. He had a cloth briefcase in one hand. A couple of younger kids flanked him, but he walked a little ahead of them.

The kid made straight for the old red car.

"Eh, Billy Grouard," said Du Pré.

Billy stopped and he looked at Du Pré, a quick glance.

"I am a friend, Jeanne Bouyer," said Du Pré, "I need talk to you."

Billy set his briefcase on the hood of the old red car. He looked at Du Pré. He waited.

The two younger boys stood behind Billy. They glared at Du Pré.

"What you want talk about?" said Billy, "Danny, he is dead. His mother, that Jeanne, she blame me now?"

Du Pré shook his head.

"You got a minute," said Du Pré, "I buy you a coke, a hamburger maybe."

Billy Grouard looked for a long moment at Du Pré.

He nodded.

Du Pré motioned him to come to the old cruiser.

Billy put his briefcase in the old red car and he came. He went round to the passenger side and he got in.

"Joe, Henry, they send you," he said.

"I ask them if Danny has friends," said Du Pré. "They say you."

Billy nodded.

"Joe, Henry, they like hassling people," said Billy, "They like to do it to me but I don't let them."

"That's what they say," said Du Pré. He started the cruiser and he drove off toward the little restaurant. Billy said nothing.

They went in. There were a bunch of kids in the place ordering sodas and french fries. They were hungry and that was what they could afford.

"What you want?" said Du Pré.

"Cheeseburger," said Billy. He was slender and hungry like a very young man. Can't eat enough.

Du Pré waited till the counter cleared and he ordered three cheeseburgers and fries and a couple of chocolate shakes. The girl behind the counter looked over at Billy, very fondly.

"I bring them to you," she said.

Du Pré nodded. He went back to the table.

"Joe and Henry they think I deal dope or something," said Billy.

Du Pré grunted.

"No drugs," said Billy, "Don't like them."

Du Pré nodded.

"What I want to ask you about," said Du Pré, "Is that place where we find Danny Bouyer's body?"

Billy looked at him.

"That is not the place you guys hang out at," said Du Pré, "I need to know where the place is, you know."

Billy looked at Du Pré and he smiled.

"You pret' smart," he said.

Du Pré rolled a cigarette.

"I take you there, sure," said Billy.

Du Pré nodded.

"If you maybe buy us some beer."

❖ CHAPTER 15 ❖

O h, man," said one of the two young kids who were
    with Billy when he came out of the school, "Why you
do that?"

Du Pré smiled. There was a case of bottled beer on the
ground at his feet. He smelled the hoppy aroma. The bottles
were all smashed.

"Pret' smart," said Billy.

"I am trying to find out why Danny Bouyer kill himself,"
said Du Pré, "I don't got time, your weaseldick games, you
know."

"I tol' you he was bad," said the other kid.

"OK," said Billy, "You tol' me. So Mister Du Pré, you
wanted to see this place? Here is this place."

The were standing in a narrow little stone canyon that cut
into the prairie. It was only a hundred feet long and ten wide
and you couldn't see it until the ground opened at your feet.
You could build a fire in the bottom at night and no one
could see it.

The rock walls were covered with red painted figures,
takeoffs on petroglyphs. Soot stained one wall. There were a
few cedar logs flung up against the slackened wall. They were
very old. Indian wickiup.

Horse thieves hid here and waited for the night. If the owners of the horses found them here, though, there wasn't a good way out of this place. Probably some bones and teeth, spent bullets here in the earth. Blood washed away long ago.

"We come down here, drum sometimes, sing," said Billy, "Big deal."

Du Pré nodded.

"How long you been doin' this?" he said.

"Three years," said Billy.

"Danny stay out here?" said Du Pré, "Maybe Jeanne is drunk and he just come on out here and he stay."

Billy nodded.

"Where?"

Billy jerked his head toward the upper end of the little canyon.

Du Pré walked past him. He looked down at the faint path. No way out at the end, so the deer didn't go through here. Just the kids, maybe a coyote come, eat their shit after they are gone.

Du Pré stooped and he went under some alders. The leaves were a pale yellow. He smelled the water. A spring bubbled up from a cleft in the yellow rock. Clear cool water.

Du Pré squatted down. He looked at the little pool. No insects at the edges. No water plants. The stream from the spring was less than a foot across. It flowed over yellow gravels and then sank into another cleft of rock.

The grass at the edges of the stream were dead and brown.

No water plants.

Du Pré sighed and he rolled a smoke. He looked again. There were some brown stalks sticking out from the gravels. He reached in and he tugged and one came away, the roots withered and tough and sparse.

Du Pré smoked.

No birds here. I have not heard a bird.

No coyote tracks, badger, fox. Deer.

Du Pré stood up.

He looked around in the grass. He found an empty quart beer bottle that still had a cap screwed on to it. He rinsed it out and he filled the bottle with the water.

He went back down to Billy and his friends.

"The water is poison," he said. "You guys, you drink here?"

Billy shook his head. So did the other two.

"But Danny, he come here, stay several days," said Du Pré, "And he drinks it, yes?"

"Well," said Billy, "Nothing else to drink."

Du Pré nodded.

"You go over, this country," he said, "You need water. You make damn sure that other creatures drink that water. You look for bugs in it, minnows, water plants. We got poison springs all over. Arsenic. Maybe something else, I don't know."

"Poison?" said Billy.

"Comes up out of the earth," said Du Pré.

Billy looked embarrassed.

"I never know that," he said.

Du Pré spat at a wolf spider scurrying through the grass stems.

"Danny he was out here a lot," said Du Pré.

Billy nodded. "His mother, she get drunk, boyfriend get drunk, she yell at Danny, I guess. He would come out here. School would have the cops look for him but they never found him."

Fucking right they didn't, Du Pré thought, walk over to this wrinkle in the earth and step in and disappear.

"How many of you come out here?" said Du Pré.

The two young kids looked at Billy.

Billy shrugged.

Du Pré went up the other side of the canyon. There was a wider more trampled path there. He saw something green through the brush and tag alders. A piece of a tent.

Du Pré pulled the cloth away from the mouth of the little cave.

A big drum, covered with another chunk of the green nylon.

A few wooden boxes. Du Pré looked in one. Rattles. Some feather headdresses in plastic bags.

Come out here, Du Pré thought, play at being Indians, I wonder what else they play at?

Du Pré went back and he walked past Billy and the two kids without speaking. They followed him.

When he got round the end of the canyon and he climbed up the long hill to where his cruiser was parked the kids were close behind. They didn't want to be left. Du Pré waited until they were in the car and then he started it and he headed back toward Lodgepole. He stopped in front of the restaurant without parking.

Billy and the two kids got out and they looked at Du Pré as he drove away.

Joe and Henry passed Du Pré, going in the other direction. They grinned. They both had big dark glasses on. Du Pré waved.

He gunned the engine and he headed toward the east. The little narrow two-lane highway snaked across the High Plains. Du Pré would get it up to ninety when he could see far ahead and slow when he crested hills or came on blind curves. The harvest season was on for some grains, and tractors pulling huge trailers at five miles an hour could be over any hill or around any bend.

Du Pré pulled off the road on a high bench that stood over a valley. He pissed. He rolled a cigarette and he had some whiskey. He could see the Wolf Mountains blue in the distance, their peaks white in the afternoon sun.

"Shit," Du Pré said. He turned the car around and headed back.

Jimmy answered the door when Du Pré knocked. He smiled and laughed.

"Du Pré," he said, "Jeanne, she will be back here in a week."

"Good," said Du Pré. "How is your sister?"

"She is in the kitchen," said Jimmy, "She likes it there, the kitchen."

"You said Danny was all right until a couple years ago," said Du Pré. "What did he do make you think he was not all right?"

"After he quit the basketball," said Jimmy, "He is very sad. Talks about killing himself then."

"Why he quit?" said Du Pré.

"He can't play good as he could," said Jimmy, "He said his eyes, they bother him. He go to reach for the ball and it is already past him. He shoot for the basket and don't come anywhere near."

"You got anything he wrote before he got bad?" said Du Pré.

"Sure," said Jimmy, "Some notebooks, from school." Du Pré stepped in the spare little house and he waited for Jimmy. Jimmy was gone a few minutes and then he came back with a paper grocery sack. It had several notebooks in it, cheap schoolbooks, spiral bound.

"I take these I bring them back," said Du Pré.

Mickey came out of the kitchen. She had been washing her hair and she had a towel wrapped around her head and a bathrobe wrapped around her body. She smiled at Du Pré.

"Danny," said Du Pré, "What else did he do maybe?"

"He fight a lot. Things set him off," said Jimmy. "He hit me a bunch of times, hit Mickey, hit Jeanne, too. She hit back, since she is usually drunk then, you know."

"He just start doing this?" said Du Pré.

"Yeah," said Jimmy. He looked very sad.

"Ok," said Du Pré, "I go now."

Du Pré put the bag of notebooks in the back of the cruiser. He drove back out the old highway and pushed the speed up and kept it there. The night was coming on and there wouldn't be any tractors on the road.

Du Pré sipped whiskey.

He smoked.

He drove.

❖ CHAPTER 16 ❖

What you mean, there is nothing in that water?" said Du Pré.

"The lab called and said there was nothing in the water you got but minute traces of metals, lime, and beer. Nothing toxic, nothing in a concentration heavy enough to be toxic," said Bart.

"Shit," said Du Pré, "That is a poison spring, there, I see them damn things all my life. We got some here. We got one right over there come out of the mountain wall behind your place. Good water everywhere around but that spring it has poison in it."

Bart shrugged.

They were sitting in the Toussaint Bar, having drinks. Du Pré had his whiskey, Bart had his club soda.

"Damn," said Du Pré.

"Poison spring," said Bart, "Never heard of them."

"Well," said Du Pré, "You drink from one you shit your brains out is all you are lucky, but, you spot one it don't got nothing in it. No life. No plants, no insects, fish."

"Only drink water that has visible organisms in it, right," said Bart.

"Yah," said Du Pré, "Plenty of them, acting healthy."

"Another explanation?" said Bart.

"I don't got one, now," said Du Pré. He sipped his whiskey.

Madelaine stuck her head out of the kitchen. She was filling in for the regular cook, who had a sick child.

"Du Pré!" she said, "Nice big steak. You want it rare, it will be a minute. I got to kill it first."

"I don't know how she does it," said Bart.

"What?" said Du Pré.

"What she does," said Bart.

"You don't make much sense," said Du Pré.

"Right," said Bart, "So, if the water not having anything poisonous in it doesn't make sense, maybe the question isn't right."

"Yah," said Du Pré.

"Mr. and Mrs. Weller should be here shortly," said Bart.

Du Pré nodded.

"The retired mining engineer. I don't know where Foote found him. They're driving a Winnebago with Illinois plates."

"If that Lawyer Foote likes him," said Du Pré, "It will be fine."

That Lawyer Foote, Du Pré thought, he is some guy. Manage Bart's money, all the family troubles that them Fascellis have. They had some plenty. Guy puts on a shirt out of the laundry, all the wrinkles smooth out, quick.

Save Bart's ass plenty.

A shadow passed the front window. Truck, something

tall on the street. Bart got up and he went to the front door and he opened it and looked out. He motioned to Du Pré.

A long motor home slowed and stopped a hundred yards down the street. It was the size of a small house, and had a satellite dish on the roof, lying flat. Lawn chairs stuck in a holder on the back next to the spare tire. A johnboat on the roof, upside down, a long piece of plastic drainpipe to hold the oars.

"I think that's the Wellers," said Bart. "We don't get many of these rolling condos here, anyway." The Wolf Mountains mercifully had no ski hill, or hot pots, or a lake big enough and easy enough to get to for the stinkboat trade.

The Wellers descended from the front of the Winnebago. They were both tall and spare, both white-haired and erect. They wore wool shirts and khakis and worn hiking boots. A Labrador Retriever followed them. The dog was old, gimpy, its muzzle white.

Bart and Du Pré walked toward them.

"Are you the Wellers?" said Bart.

They nodded and smiled.

"Mr. Fascelli?" said Mrs. Weller.

"Bart," said Bart, "and this is Gabriel Du Pré."

"Ah," said Mrs. Weller, "Charles thinks very highly of you. He said that you were a superb fiddler and a magnificent loose cannon."

"Are you related to Foote?" said Bart.

"Oh, yes," said Mrs. Weller, "He's my nephew, has been for years. My sister was his mother."

The four of them stood for a moment.

"Uh," said Bart, "You hungry? Thirsty?"

"Both," said Mr. Weller, "Alla would like a stiff . . . is it a ditchwater highball, that the term? . . . I'd like a martini."

"And steaks," said Mrs. Weller. "And some company," she added.

"I'll put Lefty in," said Mr. Weller. He turned and looked at the dog.

"He can come, too," said Bart, "Susan doesn't care. She likes dogs."

They went into the bar and got a table.

Susan bustled over, got their drink and dinner orders, and she welcomed them to Toussaint.

"It's so lovely here," said Mrs. Weller, "And Charles speaks of this place so fondly."

"Lawyer Foote," said Bart, "He has a first name and everything."

"I would never have guessed," said Susan, "Will he come to hunt this fall?"

"I think not," said Alla Weller, "He is grateful for the experience he once had here and feels it made him a better person. He is, however, quite firm about not repeating it."

Susan laughed and she went off.

"You're a mining engineer?" said Bart to Weller.

"Yes," said Weller, "I was for thirty years, then began my own company. I taught for twelve years. Alla is a geologist, and she taught for forty. We have had a rather earthbound life."

"Persephone is proposing, I gather," said Alla, "To grind

up the Sweetgrass Hills and extract the gold. And there seems to be some terrible problem with the water on the Fort Belknap Reservation. Heavy metal poisoning. Children."

"Persephone claims that the water has always run with metals," said Bart.

"They would," said Weller, "This is about money, about numbers. Though there are laws regulating this, if the fines, for instance, can be covered with the profits with something left over, then they will break the law and pay the fines. Or they will break the law, fight court battles, while they keep mining, lose in judgment, declare bankruptcy, and walk away. The assets won't pay for cleaning up the mess. Happens over and over."

"Pat knows that intimately," said Alla, "I believe since he has done just that."

"Twice," said Weller, "In both instances, though, the laws were wrong. No permanent damage and very little in the short term."

"You'll fit right in," said Bart, eyeing Du Pré, "you've come home."

Du Pré laughed.

"When will you look at the mine?" said Bart.

"Already have," said Weller, "Just a quick four-hour stroll through. Spent an evening in a saloon in Zortman, buying drinks. The mine is fairly straightforward, though there are a few things which I'd like to know a little more about."

Bart raised an eyebrow.

"Last year," said Pat Weller, "Persephone paid for seven discharges of polluted water from the settling ponds. Seven instances, when rain or something else overflowed the pond's capacities, and the processors."

"That's a lot."

Pat Weller twinkled.

"That's what they paid for," said Pat Weller, "Some three hundred thousand dollars in fines. But what they paid for does not at all reflect what they did."

Bart looked at Du Pré.

"In three hundred and sixty-five days," said Pat Weller, "the overflows occurred two hundred and forty-one times. Persephone was caught seven times. You see, one of the ways corporations fiddle with the laws is to remove the inspectors. A state may have laws, and an inspection department and a system of fines. But if the Legislature is prevailed upon to cut drastically the budgets of the enforcement agencies, then there is no cop there when the bank gets robbed."

"Simple and elegant," said Alla.

"Jesus Christ," said Bart.

"Bart," said Alla, "You've made some ten million dollars from Persephone. A nice profit. That's how they are *made*."

"You still have the stock, I hope," said Pat Weller.

Bart nodded miserably.

"Good," he said. "Now, having once visited the site as a slightly addled senior citizen, of substance, wife, Winnebago, and ancient dog, professing a collector's zeal for gold, I don't think my returning as a stockholder is quite what I would like to do at this moment."

"Later," said Alla, "You can do that later."

"But you could. You could ask some penetrating questions," said Pat.

Bart nodded.

"I'll provide you with them," said Pat.

Du Pré laughed.

Pat Weller handed Bart a folded sheet of paper.

"They're on that," he said.

Bart read the questions.

Susan Klein brought the steaks.

They ate.

❖ CHAPTER 17 ❖

Y ou are looking ver' good," said Madelaine. She hugged Jeanne Souyer. Jeanne hugged her back. They stood a moment.

"I maybe make it this time," said Jeanne, "That was a good place. Did a lot of thinkin'."

They were standing by Du Pré's old cruiser. The little jet that brought Jeanne flashed down the runway and jumped into the sky and was gone.

"You lose some weight," said Madelaine.

Du Pré loaded Jeanne's little suitcase into the trunk of the car. He shut the lid. Everybody got in the car.

"You want something to eat?" said Madelaine.

Jeanne shook her head.

"I want to see, my babies," she said.

"We go there right now," said Madelaine.

Du Pré wheeled out on to the old highway and he headed west toward Fort Belknap. He had the cruiser up to eighty-five before they had gone a mile.

"He drive like some mad bastard," said Jeanne.

Du Pré slowed down. She was still jumpy and shaky. The booze had had a good hold on her. She noticed things now that she hadn't for years.

Take her some time, get over this, Du Pré thought, she maybe make it this time. Maybe not. Wish her luck, it is a very tough thing.

"We do a lot, sweats there," said Jeanne, "Sing a lot. First time I tried to get the grandfathers, grandmothers to help me. They say that they will."

"Sure," said Madelaine, "Hey, you want a pop?"

Jeanne nodded. Madelaine reached over the back seat and she opened the little cooler and got a can out and she popped the tab and handed it to Jeanne.

"We got some cheese, stuff in there, you want some," said Madelaine.

"This is good," said Jeanne.

Jeanne was sitting right behind Du Pré. She was a big woman and heavy and she filled the one side of the seat.

"Wish my Danny was going to be there, too," said Jeanne. Very softly.

Madelaine reached back and touched her.

Du Pré sighed. He slowed the cruiser, there were some cattle in the barrow pits at each side of the road. They looked at him stupidly as he drove slowly past. One calf bolted and ran over the road behind the car.

"Damn dumb, them cows," said Du Pré.

"Was Mickey born deaf and dumb?" said Madelaine.

"Yah," said Jeanne, "She has never heard nothing. Didn't want to learn how to talk 'cause she read about Helen Keller's voice sounding funny."

"And Danny was OK?" said Madelaine.

"Uh-huh," said Jeanne, "Till maybe three years ago.

Couldn't sleep, he ached a lot. He'd been doing good in school but then he didn't. He started to hide a lot."

"Where he hide?" said Du Pré.

"Dunno," said Jeanne, "Me, I would be drunk, maybe my boyfriend too, we quarrel and Danny would take off. Didn't do so much in the winter, but he was gone a lot. Stayed with friends maybe."

Du Pré looked up in the rearview mirror. Jeanne's face was full of sorrow.

Poor woman has much to carry, Du Pré thought, I hope she can do it.

We all got a lot to carry.

"That Bart he is very nice man," said Jeanne, "He fly me both ways, pay for the hospital. It cost a lot of money."

"He got a lot of money," said Madelaine, "Now what you going to do when you get back?"

Jeanne laughed, a sudden barking.

"I be a dried-out drunk," she said, "Go to them AA meetings and I pray a lot. Sweat a lot. Lots of people on the res just like me, for sure. Take care of my babies."

"They are good kids," said Madelaine.

Du Pré rolled himself a cigarette. He lit it with Madelaine's butane lighter. A piece of burning tobacco flew off the end of the cigarette and down the front of Du Pré's shirt. He let it burn. It was a good-sized piece.

They drove in silence the rest of the way to Fort Belknap and the little town of Lodgepole. Du Pré stopped the car in front of Jeanne's house and he and Madelaine waited while Jeanne got out and she went up to her house and Mickey and

Jimmy came out laughing and they hugged their mother and the three of them chattered.

Du Pré and Madelaine got out and they went to the back of the cruiser and got Jeanne's luggage and waited a moment until Jeanne motioned them to come on and they went on up to the house and followed the family inside.

There was a banner welcoming Jeanne hung across the archway to the little kitchen.

"I got some good kids here," said Jeanne.

"We got to go," said Madelaine, "You let me know you need anything, eh?"

When they got back out to the cruiser Du Pré pulled the whiskey from under the seat and he had some and he offered some to Madelaine. She shook her head.

"I maybe like some wine," said Madelaine, "We go to the bar here, get something to eat before we go back. You were good, not drink that in front of Jeanne."

Du Pré laughed.

In the bar there were a few people nursing beers. Du Pré ordered cheeseburgers for them both and he had a ditch and Madelaine had some sweet wine. They ate quickly and Madelaine got up and went to the ladies' room and Du Pré smoked.

Dr. Redfield came in. He looked around the bar and saw Du Pré and he came over. He looked very tired.

"I got a kid in the hospital," he said, "Friend of Billy Grouard's. Sick, poisoned with heavy metals. I'm waiting on some lab tests but the symptoms are pretty unmistakable."

"When he get sick?" said Du Pré.

"He was brought in four days ago," said Redfield.

"Who bring him in?"

"His grandmother. The parents aren't around. Father's in Deer Lodge and the mother's on a roll in Great Falls. Happens a lot, the grandparents raise a lot of kids here."

"He going to make it?" said Du Pré.

Redfield nodded, and grimaced.

"He's got liver and kidney damage," he said, "Probably take ten, fifteen years off his life."

"I maybe talk to him?" said Du Pré.

"Could, I guess," said Redfield, "He sleeps a lot. He's pretty sick."

Madelaine came back.

"Got a kid in the hospital got metal poisoning," said Du Pré, "I like to talk to him before we go back."

"Sure," said Madelaine.

Du Pré got up. He left some money on the table. They went out together.

"I saw your old car," said Redfield, "Or I wouldn't have gone in there. I see a lot of people who do go in there a lot when they are sick from alcohol. I suppose I ought to let them enjoy themselves while they can."

Du Pré snorted.

They followed Redfield out to the little hospital. He led them inside and to a room with a single bed in it. The boy was hooked up to an IV and he was lying half-asleep, eyes closed almost shut.

Redfield looked the boy over. He nodded to Du Pré, and he and Madelaine left the room.

116

"Hey," said Du Pré, touching the kid's shoulder, "You remember me maybe? I need to talk to you."

The boy's eyes opened. He looked at Du Pré but didn't seem to recognize him.

"I am with Billy Grouard and you and another guy," said Du Pré, "We go out to that place, that little canyon."

The boy nodded.

"When you get sick?" said Du Pré.

The boy's eyes went blank.

Du Pré stared at him.

"You drink that water out there?" he said.

The boy looked at Du Pré with dead eyes.

He began to choke. He vomited.

Du Pré went out and he saw a nurse and waved to her. She came quickly. She went into the room and she shut the door.

Du Pré went up to the front of the building. Madelaine was sitting in the waiting room.

"What you find out?" she said.

"He don't talk to me," said Du Pré.

"Redfield, he left," said Madelaine, "He was pret' tired."

"We go back," said Du Pré.

They went out to the car.

❖ CHAPTER 18 ❖

You are soundin' ver' good tonight, Du Pré," said Madelaine. They were having a drink during Du Pré's break. The Toussaint Bar was packed with people all having a pretty good time. Only two fistfights on a Saturday night and both of those had been taken outside. Usually they happened in the bathroom and tore the hell out of the place.

Young cowboys on a Saturday night.

"That Bassman he get better each time," said Du Pré, "I ask him what he is doing, he say he listens to a lot of reggae."

"I like him," said Madelaine. "That Tally, he is nice, too. Poor guy. I think that he hurts all the time."

Du Pré nodded. He probably did. A wound that never healed would hurt all of the time.

"Jeanne she is going to the pow-wow in Bozeman, play that Stick Game some more. She say she is dry now and can't do it so good like she used to when she was drinking. I tol' her that is bullshit, she just want to drink so bad her mind play tricks on her."

"What she say to that?" said Du Pré.

"She laughed," said Madelaine, "She laugh real hard. She is good, I always like that Jeanne."

Pat and Alla Weller made their way through the people

118

packed tightly together and everyone shouting to be heard. Drinks were held high, so they wouldn't be jostled.

"Excellent!" said Alla, leaning toward Du Pré's ear, "I love this music. Where did you learn it?"

"Some here, some there," said Du Pré. Where do you learn music? Everywhere. Listen to it a lot, play a lot.

"The bass and accordion players aren't from here, are they?" said Alla.

"Turtle Mountain," said Du Pré, "There are always people going back and forth from Turtle Mountain to here, here to there, then up to the Red River country. Lots of music, my people play lots of music."

"When one comes to a Montana bar one expects some blow-dried crooner from Nashville on the jukebox," said Pat. "What a pleasant surprise this is. Very pleasant."

"We got a lot of them on the jukebox," said Du Pré.

"I've been over at Persephone's mine a couple of times," said Pat, "Just looking around. So far, it's about how those things go. The water impoundment seems adequate. The milling operation is the same and they are reclaiming the waste as much as it can be reclaimed. Contouring and seeding it with grasses and so forth. It looks just fine. It looks *groome*."

Du Pré sipped his drink.

"It looks so groomed that it bothers me," said Pat Weller. "It's just a little too nice. And the little flunk who squires me around is just a little too helpful. Gives me current daily production figures. They even look right."

Du Pré grinned.

"Uh-huh," Pat Weller laughed, "They're on to me."

"They could simply look in the directory of mining engineers," said Alla, "and find Pat Weller. All the acronyms after your name should tell them something."

"Some bright soul did that," said Pat, "But if there is something there, and I am sure that there is. There *always* is. They may think themselves clever enough to blind me with honesty. Any good mining company lies even if they don't have to, to stay in practice. I should know, I've owned four of them."

"Why you do this?" said Du Pré.

"Guilt," said Pat Weller, "I've made my millions. I'm a good Episcopalian. That makes me feel very guilty."

"Rot," said Alla, "It's that when the price of gold was let go the amount of ore available in the world increased to include whole mountain ranges. Whole basins. Whole *places* which have other uses. Deep mines do some damage, any mine does, but they are at least confined to rather small areas. Even the disaster that is Butte is only a few square miles. But now the mining companies have gone from necessary to menacing."

"You go to the Sweetgrass Hills?" said Du Pré.

"Yes," said Alla, "But many years ago. I wanted to ask you about the man that Bart mentioned, Big Jim Lascaux?"

"Yah," said Du Pré.

"Is he Métis?" said Alla.

"No," said Du Pré, "He is big and very ugly but he is not Métis."

"Well," said Alla, "We would like to go there soon."

"We all go," said Madelaine, "Now, Du Pré, you go play

120

that good music and you sing some for your Madelaine. You sing, these other people too but you sing one for me."

Du Pré finished his drink and he walked back to the little stage. Bassman and Tally were already set up and waiting. Bassman was polishing the strings of his bass with a chamois cloth.

Du Pré looked at Tally. He was pale and sweaty but he smiled as widely as he ever did.

Bassman started messing around with the bass lines, and Du Pré waited until he sort of recognized one and then he started in on "Boiling Cabbage." Bassman grinned at him and followed along and Tally took his breaks and did his chuff-chuff and when they got to the end Du Pré went into "The Black Water" and they played for an hour without stopping much. Each time they did there was a ripple of applause but they would be well into the next song in seconds and so the people in the bar just listened and talked to each other, mouth to ear, and the place got very warm and sweaty and smoky from all of the cigarettes.

The little dance floor was so crowded that people hardly moved, just danced very tiny steps in place.

Du Pré was going through the last few bars of the last song in the set, hot and thristy and his fingers were beginning to ache a little from all the playing when he saw Bart and Big Jim come in. Big Jim was laughing, his white teeth gleaming out of his long dark beard.

Put him in buckskins and moccasins and he look like a trapper for sure, Du Pré thought, red flannel leggins and a Hawken rifle. Bastard is big enough to eat hay anyway.

Tally was standing against the wall, slumped against it a little, his shirt sopping. His black curly hair was plastered to his head and neck and he was shaking a little. Du Pré put his fiddle away and he went to him and he stood quietly for a moment.

"Hey, Tally," Du Pré said, "You want to go and rest, man, Bassman and I, we finish. You don't look so good."

Tally nodded.

"I feel pret' poor," he said, "I go sit in my car, there, maybe you put my accordion away?"

Bassman had gone. Tally was so wobbly that Du Pré wanted to take his arm and throw it over his shoulder, but he didn't want to embarrass him.

"We've a good place to rest close by," said Alla Weller, "Why don't you come with us . . . Pat, take his other arm . . . we'll just walk on out to our motor home."

Tally looked at Alla Weller, who he'd never seen before.

"They are good people," said Du Pré, "You maybe want to soak in a tub there, Tally? They got one."

"Sure do," said Alla," and plenty of patent medicines."

"Tally," said Du Pré, "These good people, they help you out, yes?"

Tally nodded. Pat and Alla began to walk him through the side door. They looked gay and drew attention away from poor Tally.

Bassman came back.

"Tally got some clean clothes?" said Du Pré, "His wound is acting up I think."

"Yeah," said Bassman, "I will get them."

Du Pré followed him out the side door and they went to Bassman's van and Bassman unlocked it and he took out a duffel bag and a shaving kit.

"Who those people he with?" said Bassman.

"Good people," said Du Pré, "Bart's friends."

"Rich people," said Bassman, "Why they help old Tally?"

"They are nice folks," said Du Pré.

Bassman shrugged.

"We maybe do the last set together," said Du Pré.

Bassman nodded.

"I am going to get a drink," he said, "I been too good too much tonight."

He went off. Du Pré went over to the huge motor home and he knocked on the door. Alla opened it.

Tally was sitting at the kitchen table. Du Pré was surprised at how roomy the motor home was. A hallway led toward the back and he could hear running water back there.

Tally was looking a little better. Standing and playing had exhausted him. He was eating some cheese and there was a basket of fresh fruit on the table.

"We'll put Mr. Tally up," said Alla, "He's too good a musician not to have for company."

Du Pré put Tally's things by the chair.

"Thanks," said Tally.

"Thank you," said Alla, "You'll feel better."

Du Pré looked at her. She was smiling brightly but she looked a little worried.

✦ CHAPTER 19 ✦

Well, shit," said Bart, "I don't know if they can, but at the very least if they can't we'll know it's hopeless."

"I can't believe," said Alla, "That that poor man has been living with that all his life."

Be poor, you can live with a lot, Du Pré thought, you have to.

They were standing at the little airstrip. One of the little jets Bart could summon up had just flashed down the runway and was headed east toward the Mayo Clinic, with Tally on board.

"Horribly infected," said Alla, "just terrible. And that man just stood there and played the accordion."

Pat Weller and Big Jim were standing off a bit, and Big Jim was waving his hands in the air and keeping a big cigar going while he talked.

"Hey, Bart," said Du Pré, "I thank you. He's a pret' good accordion player, I could use him."

Bart nodded and he half-smiled.

"Well," he said, "If we're going to meet Dr. Stone at the dig site by evening we'd better make some tracks here."

"Make some tracks . . . " said Du Pré, "How you say that, Italian?"

124

"Shove it up your half-breed ass," said Bart.

"That is much better," said Du Pré, "Much better."

Pat Weller got in Big Jim's black truck and Bart and Du Pré and Madelaine and Alla got in Bart's Rover.

"This is wonderful," said Alla, "We don't have to listen to them the entire afternoon."

"No," said Madelaine, "We got to listen to Du Pré and that Bart, but we can tell them to shut up."

"But will they?" said Alla?

"Oh, yes," said Madelaine, "We can get them to."

Alla laughed.

They headed west toward the Sweetgrass Hills.

"Does Bart do that sort of thing all the time?" said Alla, looking slyly at him.

"Be a nice man?" said Madelaine, "Yah, he is very nice. He need a girlfriend, though."

"Christ," said Bart.

"He pay for this and he pay for that," said Madelaine, "I dunno, maybe he need a dick transplant or something. Me, I worry about him."

"Is this going to go on all the way to the Sweetgrass Hills?" said Bart.

"Yah, I think maybe so," said Du Pré, "You want to ride on the roof maybe I drive, yes?"

Bart looked off out the window, muttering.

"We're picking on him," said Alla, "What fun!"

"He needs it," said Madelaine, "We pick on him enough he go and get him a girlfriend then we have to find something else, pick on him about."

"He hasn't told you?" said Alla.

"Tell me what?" said Madelaine, "He don't tell me shit, that Bart. I got to guess it all the time. So he got a girlfriend, huh? Where is he keeping this lady, maybe in the basement his house?"

"Could I have your gun," said Bart, over his shoulder, to Du Pré, "It'll hurt less I just shoot myself now."

"He does indeed have a girlfriend," said Alla, "Very nice, too. She thinks the world of him."

"Ah," said Du Pré, "He is not around so much I should have known he has a girlfriend. Pret' stupid, me."

"Yah," said Madelaine, "He don't look like he want to kick the dog every day, what you think about that? Susan's cheeseburgers they are better now? Christ, Du Pré."

"OK," said Du Pré, "You know all these things you don't say nothing to me, eh?"

"We think you are smarter," said Madelaine, putting her hand on Du Pré's shoulder, "We forget, us women, men are not very smart."

Alla laughed and laughed. Her laughter was rich, like an old bell's tone.

"Bart!" she said, "Shame upon you! You haven't mentioned a word about your lady love!"

"You see why," said Bart.

"Well," said Alla, "She's at the dig right now and they'll be meeting her, don't you think your friends should have known?"

"No," said Bart. He was cruising along at seventy.

"This is a nice lady?" said Madelaine.

"Quite," said Alla, "I've known her for forty years. She's a cousin of mine, somewhat younger than I am. Twenty-five years, I think. She's forty-five."

"Pret' young woman for such an old man," said Madelaine.

"Will you fucking quit," said Bart, "I'm only fifty-four."

"He can buy her a good vibrator," said Madelaine. "He got a lot of money."

Alla laughed and laughed.

Du Pré grinned. He rolled himself a cigarette and he had a little whiskey from the flask in his bag. He lit the cigarette.

My turn it is next, Du Pré thought, now I know how them Métis the Sioux catch felt, first the women cut the nuts off the first Métis and the second he waits his turn but as yet it is not him so he is glad. This time maybe I roll down my window, jump out, escape.

They just come after me.

I sit here. Maybe I help.

"Benetsee he maybe got some roots or some thing help," said Du Pré.

"This is my car," Bart droned, "I can stop and burn it any time."

"Burn down that ugly house is fine," said Madelaine, "I like you then. This is a nice car."

"OK," said Bart.

"This lady she is what?" said Madelaine.

"She has three children, all grown and at school or

launched in life," said Alla, "Her name is Gretchen Kidder and she's working at the dig, doing this and that. Has a degree in Classics."

"She rich?" said Du Pré.

"Not terribly," said Alla.

"Christ," said Bart.

"Oh, well," said Du Pré, "I move my other shirt out of your place you going to have a woman in it."

"Now, just a goddamned minute," said Bart, "I just met her a couple of months ago."

"I only got the one shirt," said Du Pré, "It is not trouble, for me to move it."

"Christ," said Bart.

Du Pré turned around in the seat and he looked at the back cargo bay. There were two coolers in it. One old, one new. He lifted up the lid of the new one.

Flowers. Roses. Gladioli. The perfume swelled around the inside of the Rover.

"Mmmm," said Madelaine, "What is that nice smell?"

"Christ," said Bart.

"Damn," said Du Pré, "Lots of roses there. What is in this sack here?"

"Leave the fucking sack alone," said Bart.

"But this sack has me so curious," said Du Pré, fiddling it open. He pulled out a tan bush jacket, a light wool turtleneck sweater, and two small gift-wrapped packages.

Du Pré held up the sweater. It was of a medium size, deep red, and soft and rich.

"She got brown hair?" said Madelaine, "Black maybe?"

"Black and silver," said Alla, "Quite striking."

"Nice ass?" said Madelaine.

"Very," said Alla.

"Christ," said Bart.

"What you got in these boxes, here?" said Du Pré. He held up the boxes and he shook them. They both rattled a little.

"Bart!" said Alla, "That's jewelry. My, my, my. Now, do tell Alla all, my boy. Whatever did you get her?"

"Little pieces of crappy turquoise," growled Bart.

"He's lying," said Alla, "And we can't have that. Why don't you just tear open that paper and let us see what Bart has got Gretchen."

"Death," said Bart.

"It's courting behavior," said Alla.

"I set myself up," said Bart, "I could have died years ago."

Du Pré fished his knife out of his pocket and he slit the ribbon that went round the box. He slit the plastic tape that held the paper. He slid two little black velvet boxes out of white paper sheaths.

"Rape," said Bart.

Alla held out her hand and Du Pré gave her the boxes. Madelaine leaned over the seat and she waited. Alla paused and then she lifted the lid of the first box.

A ring, with a blue stone.

The second, a gold one with a topaz.

"Oh, Bart," said Alla, "Gretchen will love these! So quiet. So tasteful, and so where did you get them . . . ah, ah, foolish me, Tiffany's. Oh, good show."

"Ver' pretty," said Madelaine, "Now, how did you meet this Gretchen?"

"I arranged it," said Alla.

"What?" said Bart.

"My dear boy," said Alla, "If we women waited for you dumb bastards to make the first move the species would have died out millennia ago."

"Hoot," said Du Pré.

❖ CHAPTER 20 ❖

I can't say that it is here," said Big Jim, "I can only surmise that if it is in Montana at all, it would be here. The ice covered almost everything to the west. There were huge lakes at the bases of the glaciers. After things dried out and the ice retreated and the rainfall lessened the Great North Trail moved to the west. But I suspect that it was here a hundred thousand years ago. I expect it came right through here. I expect that. I expect the trail went through here for tens of thousands of years. It's down there. It may take centuries to find any evidence. But it is there."

Bart and the Wellers looked down at the dig site. People in moon suits were sifting and washing the soil for the hair samples. The moon suits prevented contaminating the hair with modern DNA.

"In mining," said Pat Weller, "The saw goes that you never know whether you are ten feet from a million dollars or a million feet from ten dollars. So you think that here somewhere are some hairs from people who came by here tens, perhaps even hundreds of thousands of years ago. That is a great question. Truly. I hope you can find an answer."

"If I did," said Big Jim, "It would only pose some more questions."

Du Pré was looking up the hill. An old buffalo trail wound up to the top. There was a whitish outcrop on the ridgeline. Probably lime-stone with a lot of salt in it. And while they were growing the buffalo ate at certain claybanks and crumbling limestone formations to gain enough calcium for their bones.

Buffalo licks.

But I have seen them, Du Pré thought, and they *chew* the stones.

Madelaine had wandered off, picking herbs. Some of them grew only in the Sweetgrass Hills. Never scraped off by the glaciers, plants from wetter times had hung on here long after they had been obliterated everywhere else on the High Plains.

Du Pré wandered back down to the little knot of people. He rolled a smoke and stood at the edge, listening idly to Big Jim talk of hair and fire and buffalo and people long, long ago. People with good minds and stone tools.

"There's a lot of gold in the world," said Alla, "just as there is a lot of aluminum in the mountains of New Hampshire and Vermont. It is just a matter of when it pays to mine."

Lots of people over that horizon, Du Pré thought, they are eating, drinking beer, driving cars, living their lives. They eat the Sweetgrass Hills someday I guess. Those bastards on their dirt bikes already tear them up plenty.

Knobbed tires had torn a path directly up to the ridge-line, across the zigs and zags of the buffalo trail. Water was carving a direct stream down the hill. The soil was bare where it wasn't altogether gone.

The wind shifted a little and Du Pré heard a faint whistling, a flute, one made of bone. The sound was like no other.

"Oh," said Du Pré, "I go there. I think that damn Pelon is there, he probably needs some food, water." He ran down the hill to the Rover and he got some bread and cheese and salami and a bottle of spring water and he went along the sidehill path to the little saddle that connected the two hills and he went up to the top and looked down on the little stream, dry now but water still moving through the earth, enough to keep the alders and willows alive.

Du Pré stopped.

The flute began again, very softly, steadily.

Du Pré walked toward where the flute seemed to be coming from.

A patch of alders, thick, where a hidden spring that did not even make it to the surface of the soil nourished a thick stand.

Du Pré peered through them. He saw Pelon leaning up against a rotten cottonwood log; one felled by beavers long ago.

Pelon fingered the flute and he bent over the mouthhole and he blew and the notes shimmered among the fluttering leaves.

Du Pré walked slowly toward him, following a deer path. He pushed the branches of the alders out of his way. He stood beside Pelon, who did not look up. The music stopped.

"Pelon," said Du Pré, "You want some food, water maybe?"

Pelon turned his head very slowly and he looked up at Du Pré. His eyes were sunken and his face drained.

"That would be good," he said. His voice was a whispering rasp.

"You been here, two weeks?" said Du Pré. Two weeks without any food, and only a little water. Some man, this.

"I been many places," said Pelon, "I would like a little food. You got some meat?"

Du Pré handed him the salami. Pelon took a knife out of his sash and he peeled away a thin slice and he put it in his mouth and he chewed very slowly. It took him five minutes till he swallowed. He held his hand out for the water. He took three small sips. His face went white and he turned to one side and he puked. Nothing came out. He heaved and he choked.

Du Pré rolled a smoke and he sat down on his haunches.

Pelon went on heaving and gasping. When he quit, sweat was running off his face. He stank. He hadn't bathed or changed his clothes since Du Pré last saw him.

Pelon drank a little more water. He pointed at the tobacco smoke drifting from Du Pré's cigarette. Du Pré rolled him one.

Pelon took the cigarette and Du Pré flipped his shepherd's lighter and Pelon touched the end of the smoke to the glowing coal on the rope. He drew a couple times and the tobacco caught.

Pelon took a deep drag and he held it down and then let

it out with a long wheezing sigh. His eyes quivered. He shut them. He put his hands down on the grass. He breathed deeply.

"You poison a holy man like me with nitrosamines, salt, nicotine, Christ, even a fucking yuppie wouldn't have it," said Pelon at last.

"I got some whiskey you want to make it perfect," said Du Pré.

"Fucking-A," said Pelon, "You know that old bastard said not to come back till it was time to come back. It's time to come back. Not that I miss my three-piece suits and my stockbroker all that much."

Du Pré laughed.

"How that old shit find you?" said Du Pré.

"He just did," said Pelon, "I was not happy and then one day there he was, right in front of me, looking at me with those damned black eyes of his that are older than the earth. Said I needed to come with him. My marriage was gone, there was money enough for my kids for a while. I just gave it all to my ex-wife and said I'd write."

"You write?" said Du Pré, grinning.

"Not yet," said Pelon, "I don't want to give the bitch the means to have me committed. She'd do it just out of spite. "Your Honor, my ex-husband has gone off to Montana where he is an apprentice medicine man and he tells me he sees things. For the good of him and our children please lock him up and pump him full of Thorazine. He's not well.""

Du Pré roared.

"Shit," said Pelon, "She has a point."

"That Benetsee he drive me crazy, years," said Du Pré.

"Yeah," said Pelon, "Well, he just loves to do that to young folks like you and me."

"You maybe eat a little more?" said Du Pré.

Pelon nodded. He had a little salami and cheese and some water. He had a sip from Du Pré's silver flask.

"Yup," he said, "Had my vision, the whole bit. Now I can go to the fucking pow-wows, read palms."

Du Pré roared.

"The sacred life," said Pelon, "Is not what most folks think. It is above all else not especially serious."

"Yah," said Du Pré, "That I learn from Benetsee."

"Why haven't you ever just shot him?" said Pelon.

"Me?" said Du Pré, "Oh, I think I do that plenty times but then I think about what he said, there is something in it. I am angry with myself mostly for being so stupid I cannot tell his jokes easy."

Pelon stood up slowly. He grinned at Du Pré.

"Me," he said, "I am going to go on over to that dig and I am going to take a shower, put on some clean clothes."

Du Pré nodded.

"I don't got spares," he said, "We just come for the day."

"I do," said Pelon, "They are cached right over there. Clothes, deodorant, toothbrush, fucking mousse for my hair." He walked over to a thick batch of bushes and he pulled a green ditty bag out of them.

They walked back along the trail that Du Pré had come over on. Pelon seemed fine and strong, though his filthy clothes flapped on him and his pants kept slipping down. He finally stopped and made another hole in his belt with his knife and he cinched the belt tight.

"I could market this," he said, "think of it. The Shaman's Fat Farm. Come all ye lardassed New Agers. I will bung you into the worst country and leave you there until starvation and dehydration bring useful visions and by the bye you won't have to buy your clothes from tentmakers any more. I could make millions."

Du Pré nodded.

"Starvation and dehydration, denial, better than those pills you all gobble," said Pelon, "Worked for millennia. The visions are pretty useful, of course."

"Your visions are good?" said Du Pré.

"Superb," said Pelon, "And just as soon as they reveal what the fuck they meant I can call you and mess with your head."

"Where is that Benetsee?" said Du Pré.

"Drinking screwtop wine and eating deer meat," said Pelon, "and when he belches, heaven takes notice."

"You got a lot, college?" said Du Pré.

"Oh, yeah," said Pelon, "But don't hold it against me. I didn't learn anything worth shit there."

CHAPTER 21

Fire on the mountain," said Piney. He was holding up a ripe calf head. Two of them, actually, joined at the neck. "This lovely critter came forth two days ago. Died immediately."

"Them things happen every once in a while," said Du Pré.

"Oh, shit yes," said Piney, "But I had three of them on one ranch. Big ranch, five thousand head running, statistically it can't happen."

"Jesus," said Bart.

"Rest of the little darlin' is in my freezer," said Piney, "You can send it on to that lab."

"Christ, Piney," said the woman behind the bar, "Will you get that thing out of here. It stinks like hell."

"Yah, yah, yah," said Piney, "You got a lot of customers smell a hell of a lot worse than this."

"They just smell dirty," said the woman, "That smells dead."

Piney chuckled and he went on outside. In a couple of minutes there was a sound of glass breaking. In a couple more minutes he came back in. He was laughing hard.

"Shit," said the woman behind the bar.

"I need a beer," said Piney.

"You need a goddamned cage," said the woman behind the bar.

Someone was outside cursing at the top of their lungs.

"It's just Norris," said Piney, "You know Norris."

"I do," said the woman behind the bar, "Pay up."

Piney took a roll of bills out of his jeans and he peeled off three hundred-dollar bills and he put the roll back and he turned and faced the door just as a very angry man burst through it.

"You son of a bitch!" the man said. He ran toward Piney and he jumped at him swinging. The two men crashed into the bar. Some glasses fell off the shelving near the mirror and they broke.

Piney and the man were rolling around the floor punching each other and biting and kicking.

"I don't believe this," said Bart.

Piney kneed his opponent in the nuts. The man folded up in pain.

"Is that Norris?" said Du Pré, pointing down at the groaning man.

"Yup," said the woman behind the bar, "Don't worry, they ain't done yet."

Piney was standing at the bar, dishevelled and drinking his beer.

Norris got up and hit him on the back with a chair. Norris was not feeling well, he had been aiming for Piney's head.

Piney hunkered down and Norris kicked him in the stomach and Piney folded up and fell.

139

"A beer, please," said Norris.

The woman behind the bar drew him one. Norris drank it, smacking his lips.

Piney bashed Norris in the foot with one of the legs from the chair Norris had broken over Piney's back. Norris yelped in pain and grabbed his foot and hopped.

Piney came up off the floor and he got Norris on the button with a haymaker and Norris folded up and fell with a hard thump. He lay still.

"Lying son-of-a-bitch," said Piney.

"How long this been going on?" said Du Pré.

"Thirty years," said the woman behind the bar, "The only doctor in seventy miles, maybe a hundred, and the only vet. Thirty years they been doing this. Though if anyone tried to break 'em up the two old bastards would kick the shit out of them, before going back to beating on each other."

"He's a doctor?" said Bart.

"Good one, too," said Piney, "He's stitched me up a bunch of times. Delivered all six of my kids. Saved my wife's life."

Norris groaned and stirred. He sat up, holding his head.

Piney grinned at the woman behind the bar.

"That's all for today," he said, "Could I have my change now?"

She took one of the hundred-dollar bills and she put it in the register after totting up sums on a scratch pad. She gave Piney some change.

"I had to redecorate once," she said, "But they were younger then."

"OK OK," said Piney, grinning, "We can go now, look at this clubhouse or what the hell."

Du Pré and Bart and Piney went out and they got in Bart's Rover and they drove off.

"Thought you got the water tested from this place," said Piney.

"Yah," said Du Pré, "There wasn't much in that."

"Well," said Piney, "We at least have some sterile sample bottles."

"It bothers me," said Du Pré, "This place look like a poison spring, you know, but then the water is not poison. Then, there are things about it that don't look like a poison spring. There are roots in the bottom. They are dead, but they would not be in the bottom of a poison spring at all. I don't know."

Piney nodded.

"Well," he said, "There would be sick animals, but then they go off and hide to die. So you wouldn't probably see them. You remember when they used to poison coyotes with thallium?"

"Jesus," said Bart.

"Great stuff," said Piney, "then they went to sodium fluoroacetate, which was worse. Idea was kill every coyote. Well, the coyotes did survive, and so did everything else, but in pretty damn small numbers. You ever see a coyote that had been poisoned by thallium? Takes them a month to die. All the hair falls off, the pads on their feet fall off, they go blind, they bite at themselves, die in convulsions at the end. The fluoroacetate, they just die, slowly. 'Course it killed the skunks and the badgers and weasels and vultures and magpies and rodents and anything else ate the coyotes. And then after they were dead it killed anything that ate them."

"That's illegal now," said Bart.

"So's cocaine," said Piney, "Don't mean that they can't buy it. Lots of it made in Mexico, shipped over here. Hell of a black market. I saw a field some bastard had set a couple poisoned sheep carcasses in and there were twenty bald eagles lying there dead."

Piney fished a can of beer out of his jacket pocket. He popped the top and sucked the foam down before it could spill on him.

"These kids they have a fort down there, some damn thing?" said Piney, "Lay up there, jerk off, take their girl-friends out there and play doctor, drink beer. All that good kid stuff?"

"No," said Du Pré, "I think they drum, sing, maybe get away from home. Some of their families pretty sad and crazy."

"Spring just comes out of the ground?" said Piney.

"Yah," said Du Pré, "It is in this little draw, little canyon. It is one of those places, like the earth was cut with a knife. You cannot see it if you are fifty feet away. Narrow."

Piney nodded and he sucked his beer. Bart turned on the radio and they listened to country music and ads for snoose and beer. Cars.

"It is there," said Du Pré, pointing off in the flat pasture. There was no fencing here, it was open range, meaning it was too poor to pay to fence.

Bart drove slowly over the rough country. He stopped when Du Pré tapped his shoulder.

They got out and Du Pré led them over to the little canyon. There was fall color in the leaves of the bushes and the cottonwoods were bright yellow. Du Pré found the path and he led them down. Piney was carrying a bright red bag. The plastic bottles in it thumped together.

At the bottom Du Pré turned right and he headed up the path to the place where the spring bubbled up. He looked down and saw a few signs that Billy Grouard and his friends had been back.

Du Pré stopped and he looked down at the yellow jumbled rock where the water came out clear and sparkling. A couple of water striders were darting across the surface.

Du Pré frowned. They hadn't been there before.

Piney had dropped down to his haunches and he was staring at the bottom of the little stream that flowed out of the spring and then dived beneath the earth.

Piney reached down and he grabbed one of the brown roots and he tugged it free. Mud and water dripped into the grass.

Piney dipped out a bottle full of water.

"OK," he said, "What we do is get this mud."

Du Pré knelt to help.

They crammed eleven bottles full of muds. Some from the bottom near the spring, some from near where the water sank back into earth.

"This was poison all right," said Piney, "But it ain't now, I'll bet. So let's have that fancy lab see what they can find. If they find what I expect, we'll want to come back and take cores."

"Cores," said Bart, "Why?"

"Well," said Piney, "If the stream was once poison and now it ain't, it would be nice to know when it changed."

A magpie flew down from the cottonwood tree where it had been perched. It flew past Du Pré and Piney.

And it flew into the rock wall and fell to the ground and it fluttered some and lay on its back.

"That magpie would know," said Piney, "But for him it's too late."

CHAPTER 22

This awful kind of you," said Jeanne, from the backseat of the old cruiser. She was wearing a beautiful beaded shawl.

"We want to go to that pow-wow anyway," said Madelaine, "It is a ver' big one, that Bozeman one."

Du Pré looked off at the sagebrush. He did not want to go to the pow-wow. He never wanted to go to Bozeman, which he hated. Fat and smug. And any Indian pow-wow which "celebrated cultural diversity" was using long words where short ones would do, and thinking short thoughts where long ones were needed.

"You never been this one, Du Pré?" said Jeanne.

"No," said Du Pré.

Me, I have this perfect record, Du Pré thought, and now it is gone, pouf, like that.

"It is in that field house," said Jeanne, "Huge place, where they have the basketball and the rodeo."

And the rock bands and what all shit, thought Du Pré. I hate that Bozeman. Too much bad money there. All piled up. Lots of ugly houses out on the foothills.

Used to be a pret' nice place.

Long time ago.

"Where you stayin'?" said Jeanne.

"Hotel over in Livingston," said Du Pré. A ratty place full of winos and guys just got out of Deer Lodge, well, not any more, but Du Pré remembered it when it was interesting.

"Good Stick Games," said Jeanne, "Me, I hope I can do this. It would be good for me, do this well."

"You do good," said Madelaine. "They got that Kiowa team this place now?"

"Yah," said Jeanne, "They are plenty good, too."

Du Pré was roaring down the highway between Harlowtown and Big Timber, past the Crazy Mountains on his right.

They were beautiful, rising out of the High Plains alone. Crazy Peak up there at eleven thousand feet.

Du Pré looked at some black thunderclouds over in the west, on top of the Bridger Mountains. It rained in Bozeman quite a lot. They were at the east end of a long valley and the clouds piled up against the mountains and dumped as they lifted to go over. Twenty inches of rain a year, pretty good for Montana.

The road was potholed and very narrow. Du Pré dodged some of them and others he thumped through.

When they got to the Interstate they stopped at a gas store and pissed and Du Pré got some tobacco and pop. The stupid young woman at the cash register punched in something wrong and the register wouldn't open and Du Pré finally told her to keep the twenty-three cents and he went back out to the cruiser and they went on. The Interstate was full of huge trucks driving very fast. The speed limits had been raised again.

The Yellowstone flowed past on the right as they headed west. It was low and green with algae.

"That used to be pret' clean," said Madelaine, "Long time ago."

Fly fishermen farted around in expensive drift boats. There were people in canoes paddling downstream.

When they got to Bozeman Du Pré made his way up toward the campus and the huge field house. There were hundreds of cars and trucks there, in the lots, and streams of people headed toward the doors. Du Pré stopped and he got Jeanne's luggage out of the trunk. She picked up her few things from the back seat and then she and Madelaine hugged.

"You be back now?" said Jeanne.

"We see you tonight," said Madelaine, "We go back to the hotel and we get something to eat and we drive over. Livingston is only twenty-five miles from here, not far."

"Yeah," said Jeanne, "We just pass it. I am sorry."

"Next time you can move Livingston to the other side of Bozeman," said Madelaine, "For now it is OK though."

They laughed. Du Pré and Madelaine drove off.

"I am hungry," said Du Pré, "Maybe there is some place to eat here in this Bozeman."

They drove along the main street. Boutiques, expensive little restaurants. Delicatessans. A bagel factory.

"There is no place here to eat," said Madelaine, "Hey, that kid with the green hair there!"

Du Pré looked over. The kid had plastered some sort of green stuff in his hair which stood up like a fin on his head. He had a lot of jewelry on and black leather clothes.

"Me," said Du Pré, "I can't eat a place like this."

They drove to Livingston and found a good restaurant and ordered steaks. The place was quiet and clean and the steaks were good and it didn't cost all that much.

They checked into the hotel and rode up to the third floor on an old elevator. The room was small but clean and there was a big soft double bed.

"Feel better now, eh, Du Pré," said Madelaine, later. "I know you don't want to go, that pow-wow. I got to for Jeanne."

"We go maybe tomorrow," said Du Pré.

"I want to go," said Madelaine, "What can we do here, Livingston? Find some dumb rock band, listen to it?"

"OK," said Du Pré, "I go."

They showered and dressed and drove back over the hill. They found a place in the parking lot and left the ragged old cruiser and they walked to the field house. There was a ten-dollar admission. Du Pré shrugged and he paid it.

The field house was full of exhibits and one end of the huge arena was given over to the traders. There were fancy-dancers circling slowly one end of the wooden basketball floor. A singing society sat around a huge drum and sang the old ululations.

That is a very old sound, Du Pré thought, long time gone.

They wandered through the knots of people watching

the fancydancers. Du Pré looked around for Jeanne but he didn't see her. He was staring off at a group of people in the stands when Madelaine grabbed his arm.

"Du Pré!" she hissed, "There is Jeanne, she is drunk I think."

Jeanne was standing near one of the doors that went back to the shower rooms with several other women. Jeanne and one woman as big as she was were faced off and shouting at each other.

Madelaine dragged Du Pré along.

Madelaine let go of Du Pré's arm and she started to run.

Jeanne and the other Indian woman circled each other and then they closed and began to fight. The other women began to scream and yell.

Du Pré glanced over to his right. A couple policemen were running toward the brawl. More women joined in. There were eight or ten now, pounding each other.

Madelaine stopped twenty feet away, yelling.

The women went on until the cops came and they began to push people apart and yell, too.

The fight stopped and some of the women began to walk away.

Jeanne and the woman she had been fighting stood sullenly while a big policeman talked to them.

Jeanne was swaying a little and her face was bloated and red.

She looked for a long time, stupidly, at the cop.

Then she took a swing at him.

His partner joined him and they took Jeanne down and they handcuffed her and they lifted her back up and began to walk her away toward a door that led out of the arena.

Du Pré came up behind Madelaine.

"We go bail her out," he said.

"No," said Madelaine, "We don't do that. Poor Jeanne, but if she won't take no help we can't help. Poor Jeanne. What happen to her."

"She is maybe afraid about the Stick Game," said Du Pré.

"Something," said Madelaine, "Look, Maybe we just go look at the things the traders have a little, go back to the hotel, listen to some dumb rock band and get some sleep. I call the jail in the morning."

Du Pré nodded. Jeanne would at least be sober by then.

"I am sorry," said Du Pré.

Madelaine shrugged.

They walked around the booths, looking a little, but it was all cheap trade jewelry and other junk. Beaver skins. Bad quillwork and beadwork. Tourist stuff.

They went back out to the car.

Back at the hotel in Livingston they had a couple drinks in a horrible bar on the first floor. The place was new and ugly, with a big island in the middle of it.

Du Pré remembered the old bar. He had been having a beer in it when he was just back from the service, before getting his bus home.

Two cowboys had got into a fight then and the other patrons didn't bother to look up. But that was a long time ago.

❖ CHAPTER 23 ❖

Hey," said Madelaine to Jeanne, "You fuck up once it is OK. So what? You go home now, you feel better in awhile, start again, eh?"

Jeanne was sitting in the back seat of the cruiser. Du Pré was shooting along the potholed blacktop. Flickertail ground squirrels darted out of the way of the car. Every once in a while a squashed flickertail stuck to the blacktop, for being slow.

"I am so ashamed," said Jeanne, "Dumb damn Indian, I go there, you drop me off, I walk down to where I can get some liquor. I don't walk, that is a lie, I take a cab, take a cab back. Sneak the bottle in, it is not hard, drink in the bathroom, drink back in the halls under the seats. Lots of places do that there."

"So," said Madelaine, "You will do better."

"I did not do better," said Jeanne, "I am sorry, I think I am going to be sick again."

Du Pré braked and he got off on a dirt track that went out to a grain field yellow gold with ripe wheat. Jeanne struggled out and she puked for a while, her hand on the rear fender of the cruiser. Madelaine stood by her, patting her shoulder.

"You drink some more pop," said Madelaine, "It will make you feel better."

"Only thing make me feel better is a drink," said Jeanne, "That is the only thing."

"Du Pré give you a little of his whiskey then," said Madelaine.

Du Pré reached over the seat and he got her can of pop and he pulled the whiskey from under the seat and he poured an ounce or so into the can. He handed it out to Madelaine, who gave it to Jeanne.

Jeanne drank it. She stood heaving a little but it stayed down.

"You be better now," said Madelaine, "Listen, we get to Lodgepole you maybe go to the hospital, that Dr. Redfield maybe help you not feel so bad you are drying out."

Jeanne nodded miserably.

She got in and so did Madelaine. Du Pré wheeled out on the road again. He sipped some whiskey from the bottle. He rolled himself a smoke one-handed.

My father, that Catfoot, Du Pré thought, he say the only really bad thing about jail is that you can't get a drink in it. He is there plenty, my papa. Fight a lot. Get stopped by cops and fight them. Couple times he win and they pick him up later. My mama mad as hell at him, she yell a lot about how he is a no-good drunken Métis son-of-a-bitch always getting in trouble.

Catfoot just grin at her, say, yeah, but I got a big dick.

He say that once too often, she knock him cold with a bread mixing bowl, tie him up with clothesline, beat the shit out of him, a broom handle, he limp a few days, stitch here and there. He get arrested again but he don't say that no more.

"What you laughing at, Du Pré?" said Madelaine.

"Think of my Papa, Catfoot," said Du Pré, "Him in jail plenty."

"Yah," said Madelaine, "Well, you act like him some but not enough to get put in jail. Maybe someday I whip your ass like your mama did Catfoot."

"Probably," said Du Pré.

"I have some more whiskey," said Jeanne, "You are right, I go to the hospital."

Du Pré shrugged and he handed Madelaine the bottle.

She gave a can of pop a charge and handed it to Jeanne.

"Where you get all that damn money?" said Madelaine, "You bail yourself out, Jeanne, you still got a thousand dollars left? You win big, the Stick Game you don't play?"

Jeanne looked out the window.

"I don't talk, my money," she said.

"You got too much money to explain, poor woman like you," said Madelaine, "Me, I want to know about that."

Jeanne put her head down and she sucked on the can of pop.

"That fool Bart give it to you?" said Madelaine, "He think hundred-dollar bills are toilet paper."

"Yah," said Jeanne, "He try to help me out, say please don't tell any body he is doing it."

Madelaine nodded.

"He was trying to help," said Madelaine.

"Shit," said Jeanne. She finished her pop and looked at the can.

"We make a deal," said Madelaine, "You have what you want, but you go to the hospital first we get back."

Jeanne nodded.

"Damn life just go poof like that" said Jeanne, "Mickey she is born, can't hear, can't talk. Danny he is a good kid but he is slow, then he get all sad. He shake a lot. Can't hold a pencil sometimes. Then he kill himself. Jimmy he is a sweet kid he is slow too. That damn ex-husband of mine, he is drunk or stealing things. No help. Some of them places we live, awful, no running water, broken windows, shacks, all wrecked."

Madelaine nodded. A lot of people on the reservation lived like that. It was all that they had or expected.

"Danny is slow in school?" said Madelaine, "I thought he did pretty good."

"I mean the last couple years can't pay attention. I go talk to the teachers, they say he can't read a book, tell you what's in it. Can't play basketball."

Jeanne dug another can of pop out of the cooler and she popped the top and she sucked out a few swallows and she handed it to Madelaine. Madelaine handed it back and gave her the whiskey bottle. Jeanne looked at her and she tipped the whiskey up and drank deep and then choked a little and she chased the shooter down with some soda.

They rode in silence the rest of the way and Du Pré drove up to the hospital and Jeanne got out and Madelaine helped her inside. Du Pré sat and waited, having some whiskey and smoking.

The sun was bright and the day warm. Du Pré got out and he walked down to a little irrigation feeder and he ducked behind some hay bales piled near it and he took a leak. He glanced down at the irrigation channel. It needed cleaning.

He wandered back to the cruiser and he dug out some bread and cheese and he ate, drinking a can of soda.

Madelaine and Dr. Redfield came out of the hospital. Their heads were down and they were talking. Redfield scratched his head. Madelaine stopped and she waved her hands for a while and then they came on.

"Hi Gabriel," said Dr. Redfield, "Jeanne's resting. We'll get her detoxed in a couple of days. Fell off the wagon in Bozeman, huh?"

Du Pré shrugged.

"He say that Mickey and Jimmy are doing fine," said Madelaine, "I think they don't need Jeanne. It hurts her."

"Well," said Redfield, "She wasn't there for them much when she was drinking or drugging. So they grew up on their own. They're nice kids. I'll go by and see them this evening when I am through here."

"We got to get back to Toussaint," said Madelaine, "But we come back soon. We don't stop at Mickey and Jimmy's today. You call them? Let them know where Jeanne is?"

"I'll go by there," said Redfield.

Du Pré and Madelaine got in the cruiser and they drove

155

off. It was almost three hours to Toussaint and they would be pressing night by the time that they got there.

Madelaine mixed a little whiskey in a can of pop and she had that. She looked out the window and she didn't speak.

Du Pré smoked and sipped whiskey while the sagebrush country rolled past. Antelope dashed away, their rumps brilliant white.

"I don't know what Jeanne can do," said Madelaine, "She goes down to Bozeman for the Stick Game and she gets drunk, gets arrested. Them other women they won't have that much. Jeanne was good but she isn't anymore. So she blows up. I think maybe she go there and they say they don't want her maybe."

Du Pré rolled a cigarette.

"I like to talk to those other women," said Madelaine, "Don't know who they are though."

"Redfield would know," said Du Pré.

"Maybe," said Madelaine, "But maybe not. Lots of people won't go to that hospital."

Du Pré nodded.

"Nothing ever go right for her," said Madelaine, "Kids got troubles, she got them, nothing ever go right. She was such a pretty woman. Good kind heart. I remember her then."

"She is lying to you some," said Du Pré.

"Eh?" said Madelaine.

"Bart don't give her no thousand dollars all at once," said Du Pré, "Bart knows better. He is a drunk, too. He pay her hospital, maybe he give her a hundred bucks for groceries.

But he knows better than to give her a bunch of money. Bart, he would not do that."

"OK," said Madelaine, "We ask him make sure though."

"If it is not Bart," said Du Pré, "It is someone though."

"Who the hell give her thousands of dollars it is not Bart?" said Madelaine.

Du Pré nodded. He had a drink.

✤ CHAPTER 24 ✤

Du Pré bumped up the rutted road to Benetsee's cabin. There was an ancient pickup truck, the paint all gone to soft red rust, parked off in the tall rank grass. A big yellow dog shot out of the front door and over the porch and leaped off and woofed up to Du Pré's car. The dog stopped barking when he got close, and began to wag his tail. The dog grinned, too.

Du Pré got out and he patted the dog on the head.

The dog lifted a leg and pissed on Du Pré's boot.

"Yah," said Du Pré, "You belong here, I guess."

He walked up to the cabin and he looked through the open door. There wasn't anyone inside that he could see.

Du Pré heard a tapping behind him. He turned. Benetsee was by the cruiser, tapping on the glass with his long fingernail.

"Old man!" said Du Pré, "It is good to see you! Such a long time I have gone without your bullshit! I have brought you wine! Meat!"

Benetsee grinned, the stumps of his old teeth yellow-brown.

"You are older, Du Pré," said Benetsee, "But not very smart yet."

Du Pré opened the trunk and he took out a jug of screw-top wine and a pint jar and he opened the wine and filled the jar and he handed it to the old man. Benetsee drank it down in a long swallow. He waited for Du Pré to finish rolling him a cigarette.

Du Pré lit it and gave it to him.

"Your manners better these days," said Benetsee, "So what you want?"

"You haven't been around, so long, I forgot," said Du Pré, "Maybe I ask that Pelon."

"Yah," said Benetsee, "Pelon, he is much more patient with fools than I am. He don't got so many of them piles, makes me mean."

"He in the sweatlodge?" said Du Pré.

"Taking a bath," said Benetsee, "Medicine man take a bath, he lose strength, I tell him. He say I am plenty strong for both."

"You buy a bathtub?" said Du Pré, "What is this? You get a dishwasher next."

"He get one. He put it back by the sweat. Build a fire under it, heat it up all nice. Put herbs in it. Sit in it. Smell like stew meat."

"Madelaine says come and eat," said Du Pré.

Benetsee held out the jar for more wine.

"That's better than this talking to you," he said, "That Madelaine is a smart lady. What she want with you I can't tell. Maybe I come, eat, we talk about that."

"She love me," said Du Pré.

"Yah," said Benetsee, "Yah, she need me all right. Now

159

what you want to know about them Sweetgrass Hills. Pretty good place. I got a wife buried in them, down by where the old people come at night to the water."

Du Pré nodded. Benetsee drank wine.

"Them old people eat them elephants, them buffalo got the long horns," said Benetsee, "Funny animals, all too big. We eat them all long time ago."

Du Pré rolled himself a cigarette. He smoked for a while. Benetsee had some more wine.

"Kid died on the Fort Belknap Res," said Du Pré, "son of Madelaine's cousin. I found him, he was pretty rotten you know. He was a good kid, then he got sick a couple years ago, sick in the head, I think."

Benetsee nodded.

"Other kids are sick, too," said Du Pré, "Something in the water maybe. I don't know."

"OK," said Benetsee, "Where does Red River start?"

Du Pré shrugged.

"Starts uphill from where it is Red River," said Benetsee, "It can flow under the earth, you know. Same with the others."

"That mine poisons the water," said Du Pré, "But how? I go and take some of the water, the spring where this kid hides out, it is fine."

"You look at that creek," said Benetsee, pointing to the little stream that ran in back of his house.

"Yah," said Du Pré.

"Sometimes it is clear," said Benetsee, "Sometimes it is pret' muddy."

"OK," said Du Pré, "You come and eat then."

"We come this evening," said Benetsee, "I talk to that poor Madelaine. She is in a lot of trouble, you know."

"Yah," said Du Pré.

"I come over there the Sweetgrass Hills couple days," said Benetsee, "I want to talk to that Big Jim."

"Sure," said Du Pré. "He would be honored."

"He is a good man," said Benetsee, "Tries to understand."

Du Pré nodded, not knowing what Benetsee meant, exactly, but then he never did, exactly.

"OK," said Benetsee, "You go away now. I got things to do."

Du Pré drove off. He stopped before he got on the blacktop and he watched a big yellow-gray coyote eat grasshoppers for a while. The coyote would only eat the grasshoppers that flew.

God's Dog, there, Du Pré thought, playing. I like them damn coyotes, kill enough of them. Pelts aren't worth anything any more, people think fur is a bad thing. My people are made by fur. The fur trade. Us voyageurs. Paddle them canoe, haul fur for the Hudson's Ray Company. Long time ago.

Du Pré dumped the last few flakes of tobacco from the pouch in his shirt pocket into a paper and made a skinny cigarette. He wheeled out on to the blacktop and headed for Toussaint.

Susan Klein was sitting on a stool in front of the bar. There was no one else in the place. She had been cleaning and her head was bound with a blue railroadman's handkerchief.

"A customer," she said, "Damn, could you come back in an hour?"

"I am out of tobacco," said Du Pré, "I get it and write it down."

"I told you I had a century's supply in the freezer," said Susan, "I don't know why it was bought. I'd be as happy you just took it all away, except for a hundred packs."

"But I don't got so big a freezer," said Du Pré.

"Right," said Susan Klein.

"Benetsee is back," said Du Pré, "He has been gone more than he is here, couple years."

"I'd love to see him," said Susan, "Sometimes I think he's older than the land. Does anyone know what tribe he is from?"

Du Pré shrugged. He didn't know.

"Maybe Cree," said Du Pré, "Maybe he is just a Métis, I don't know."

"He's a good friend," said Susan, "I feed him when he comes, but he does that so seldom."

Du Pré went to the freezer and he got a dozen bags of tobacco. Good old Bull Durham.

Du Pré mixed himself a ditchwater highball and he took the glass around the bar and he sat next to Susan.

"How's Madelaine?" said Susan.

"She is good," said Du Pré.

"And Tally? He has surgery?"

Du Pré nodded. "I don't hear how he is yet," he said.

The door opened and Bart came in, with the old hand Booger Tom who pretty much ran Bart's ranch and Bart, too.

"The boss is in love," shouted Booger Tom, "and the sheep ain't so nervous."

"Christ," said Bart.

"I tell him to go the hell over to the archy-ologees and make nice with the woman," said Booger Tom, "But he'd rather mope around like a sick pup, pissing himself and looking sorrowful."

"Afternoon, Tom," said Susan, "I see you're feeling well."

"I am that," said Booger Tom, putting the cane he always used now up against the bar, "Man gets to be my age and finds himself not dead it pleases him."

"If nobody else," said Susan, going around the bar, "What'll you have?"

"Fancy drink," said Tom, "Whiskey with a little sody water in it."

Susan nodded. She made up his drink and she drew a tall glass of club soda for Bart.

"Hey Bart," said Du Pré, "I talk to you a minute?" He walked away from Susan and Booger Tom and he waited for Bart to catch up to him.

"You didn't give Jeanne Bouyer a bunch money, did you?" said Du Pré.

Bart shook his head.

"She was just out of spin-dry," said Bart, "Bad idea. No, I didn't give her anything. I gave her a couple hundred so she could buy cigarettes and snacks while she was in the hospital, but nothing since. I guess she lost it down in Bozeman."

"She had a lot of money," said Du Pré, "Couple thousand said she got it from you."

"Nope," said Bart, "And whoever gave it to her was probably trying to get her to fuck up."

"Who would do that?" said Du Pré.

"Jeanne knows," said Bart.

"I call that Redfield maybe," said Du Pré, digging in his pockets, for a quarter.

Bart handed him a cellular phone.

"I can guess who," said Bart.

"Me, too," said Du Pré.

✤ CHAPTER 25 ✤

S weet Christ," said Pat Weller, "Of course they do things like that. We live in a capitalist world, Du Pré. Lie, cheat, steal, profit. I of course heartily approve. It's been damned good to me. No other system devised by man has provided so many good things for so many people. But it does have its dank folds and hideous absolutes."

"Yah," said Du Pré, "Maybe that Jeanne tell us who that is though."

"Hardly matters," said Pat Weller, "Since some third assistant under-flunky would deliver the money anyway."

Bart and Pat and Alla Weller and Du Pré and Big Jim were standing at the dig site in the rain. The rain was gentle and steady and looked fair to go on for the rest of the day.

"Persephone is part of a conglomerate," said Pat Weller, "a little part at that though they make a couple billion dollars a year off the various mines, they have them all over the world. Profit profit profit. And I think I may have an answer about poor Danny Bouyer, too."

Du Pré looked at him.

"If the weather breaks we can fly over the mine," said Pat, "There's a couple buildings there which don't make any sense to me."

"The whole damn thing don't make sense to me," said Du Pré.

"Next knot in the oil supply gold will hit a thousand dollars an ounce," said Pat Weller, "That's a lot of sense. Not good poetry but fine investments."

Du Pré shrugged.

"They're here," said Big Jim. He was squinting up at the ridgeline. There were two figures standing on it.

Benetsee and Pelon.

They slouched loosely and they seemed to be dressed in old patched clothes.

"Christ," said Bart, "Our medicine men look like garden-run winos."

"The short one, him, he is," said Du Pré sourly. He had a jug of screwtop wine in his bag and extra tobacco and some dried meat and fruit that Madelaine had sent.

That old bastard make plenty fun of me now, Du Pré thought, but then I am pretty funny and not so smart anyway.

Big Jim started to walk up to the two and the others followed. It took about ten minutes to make the climb. The grass was slippery and wet and bootsoles slipped on it.

Benetsee grinned at everyone. He walked over to Big Jim and looked up at the giant man. Jim smiled and held out his hand and Benetsee took it and they shook a moment.

"Pret' nice day," said Benetsee, "Any water here, pret' nice day."

Du Pré looked at Pelon. He had on some expensive hiking boots that were of a light construction of nylon cloth. They had moccasin soles with no arch or heel. Benetsee had on old moccasins, but some woman had beaded them beautifully. The beads glowed in the half-light.

Du Pré got Benetsee some wine and the old man drank and he waited for Du Pré to roll him a cigarette and then he smoked. The clouds broke to the west and some shafts of sunlight shot down. The rain was lifting. A meadowlark sang.

"Do you know what we are doing here?" said Big Jim, shrugging toward the dig.

"Digging in the wrong place," said Benetsee, "Is what you doing there."

Big Jim laughed and laughed.

"Where is the right place?" he said.

"Not far," said Benetsee, "They never are."

Big Jim roared and so did the Wellers.

"More wine," said Benetsee to Du Pré. Du Pré poured.

"I first see these hills," said Benetsee, "They were mountains. Me, I swam in a lake that was here. Then the ice come all around, you know, except for a tongue of land goes northeast. The trail come down from there, come down from the Land of Little Sticks. Long trail."

"The Great North Trail," said Jim, "That one?"

"Star That Never Moves Trail," said Benetsee, "Long time gone. East of China there are a people who speak some of my tongue, you know."

"Jesus," said Big Jim.

"How you know where China is?" said Du Pré.

"You don't know, your ass is, most times," said Benetsee, "I am older, know these things. These young people they don't respect old people no more. Anyway, there are old songs, you know. One goes, mountains, desert, grass, forest, water, moss, forest, grass, sweet grass. We carry the sweet grass all that way."

"What kind of water?" said Big Jim.

"Black water, rising," said Benetsee.

"Well," said Big Jim, "That'd do for the back side of the Himalayas all the way here."

"Where you think that sweet grass come from?" said Benetsee, "It is not here. We bring it, long time gone."

Du Pré nodded.

"What you see, Du Pré," said Benetsee, sweeping his arm over the rolling land. He stopped pointing down at the little watercourse that ran at the foot of the hill, where Pelon had been when Du Pré found him, starving and exhausted.

Du Pré squinted, blurring his vision so he could see big things and shadings.

"You see two colors almost alike," said Benetsee.

Du Pré nodded. Which fucking two colors?

The grass. It was one color above and another below. A ragged line ran more than halfway up the far hill. It was level, in the distance.

"There was a lake here," said Du Pré.

"Ah," said Benetsee, "More wine. Big lake, too."

"Yes," said Alla, "There's the old shoreline. Subtle but it is there surely. Do you see it, Pat?" She pointed.

"I need new glasses," said Pat, "No, I can't."

Du Pré began to walk downhill. He took a thong from his pocket and he held one end of it to his nose and the other under his thumb against his first finger. He sighted, went down another ten feet.

"Hey Bart," Du Pré yelled, "Come tell me this looks level."

Bart came. He stood to the side and he moved Du Pré's hand a little."

"I think so," said Bart.

"Go back to where the line meets the hill," said Du Pré, standing still.

Bart took a knife from his pocket and he opened it and he set it down into the soil.

Benetsee had come down, the others trailing behind.

"What you see?" he said.

Big Jim looked hard around.

"Christ," he said, "If there was an ice dam to the west the lake would drain north, through that saddle." He pointed toward a low ridge connecting two of the hills.

"This went to Red River," said Du Pré.

"It damn well did," said Big Jim.

"This lake left long ago," said Alla, "Very long ago. A lot longer ago than ten thousand years."

"I'd have thought it was too high for a site," said Big Jim.

"You're down on the old lake bottom, Jim," said Alla, "There was a smaller lake there but a lot later."

"Jesus Christ," said Big Jim.

"But it is maybe all gone," said Benetsee, "Long time ago."

Pelon was playing a flute.

Benetsee held out his jar for more wine and Du Pré filled it and he rolled the old man a cigarette.

Benetsee smoked.

"We got things, do," he said, walking downhill. Pelon trotted after him. They got to the trees and alders and they went into them and they disappeared.

Du Pré and Bart and the Wellers walked along, Big Jim was still standing staring at the saddle a half-mile away.

They stopped on top of the hill and looked over at the dig site and the people in moon suits washing the soils.

"Could I try that wine?" said Alla. Du Pré handed her the jug. She hooked an expert thumb in the handle and tipped it up and she had a good stiff drink.

"God," she said, letting the jug down, "That is *dreadful*."

"Let me try," said Pat. He swilled some and gagged.

"I think they make it of redwood bark and molasses," said Alla.

"I am getting cold," said Bart, "I'm going down for some coffee." He began to run down the hill in little steps.

"Just like that," said Alla, "I wonder if there is anything there."

"Perhaps," said Pat, "How old would you expect that shoreline to be?"

"Fifty, even a hundred thousand years," said Alla, "I'd like to know why the grass remembers."

It did only in this light, Du Pré thought, if this was a bright day it could not be seen, a darker one either. Only if the light is this can you see that line. It is getting darker now and I think maybe it can't be seen any more. But that Benetsee, he knows when it is there.

Du Pré smiled.

"Where are they going?" said Alla, "That wonderful old man."

"Get drunk, bum quarters," said Du Pré.

"Right," said Alla, and she laughed.

"Him," said Du Pré, "I never know where he goes, he just does."

"Oh, look," said Alla, pointing off toward a far hill, "There's a couple of coyotes."

CHAPTER 26

Piney's gonna probably kill one of the engineers," said Pat Weller, "The mud samples you guys got were so full of heavy metals and cyanide compounds we all hope you didn't lick your fingers clean after you filled the bottles."

"That is a long way from that mine to that little spring," said Du Pré, "So how does that stuff get all the way over there?"

"Groundwater," said Pat Weller, "And I think I know how this stuff gets in the groundwater in such concentrations. I think that the two buildings I can't find a purpose for house injection wells."

"OK," said Du Pré, "What is that?"

"Long tube down deep," said Pat Weller, "And you pump the crap down into some porous layer and you just hope it doesn't pop up anyplace very soon."

"They do this a lot?" said Du Pré.

"Oh, yes," said Pat Weller.

"I've looked at the subsurface maps of this whole region," said Alla, "They're pretty thorough. Lots of fractured rock, lots of places for the groundwater to move through. Persephone was unlucky. The injection well is at a precise elevation above the little spring you took the mud samples from. Many miles away, but there is one contiguous fissure down there and the water apparently runs right through it, like a pipe."

Du Pré shook his head.

So Danny Bouyer he come out of the old well in rotten pieces. Who are these damn people anyway?

"Bastards," said Du Pré.

"They are that," said Pat Weller, "You know that they weren't pumping into the injection well all the time. Just when something else went wrong and the overflows were large or there was some unholy concentration of metals for whatever reason. Water too polluted to make it by even the minimally inspected meters. If the overflows leached just a tiny bit more than allowable, the people monitoring it would be inclined to let it pass anyway. They need a clear batch of evidence. If, say, the evidence was just that there was an overflow, but one within the percentages, it wouldn't pay to argue that in court."

"Fuckers," said Du Pré.

"And it would have to be proven that the metals from the mine were in fact from the mine," said Pat Weller.

"Where else they come from?" said Du Pré.

"No," said Pat Weller, "Wrong question. You have to prove that the pollution came from the mine. Have to follow it all the way through the groundwater. Otherwise Persephone can point out that there is, regrettably, some pollution, which is terrible, but they aren't providing it."

173

Du Pré nodded. Whiteman law.

"So how we do that?" said Du Pré.

"I am thinking about how we do that," said Pat Weller.

"All aboard," said Piney. He'd been fiddling around with something in the cockpit of the little four-seater plane that sat out back of his veterinary hospital. The plane was dinged and scratched and some of the Plexiglas was starred and there were three bullet holes through the tail, Du Pré stared at them.

"Norris," said Piney, pointing, "Bastard hid in the ditch and waited for me to take off last year and tried to blow me out of the sky. He can't hit ducks either. Dumb bastard."

"That's attempted murder," said Alla, looking pale.

"Yah," said Piney, "Well we have done attempted that on each other from time to time. The son-of-a-bitch. Christ, he makes me mad."

"How long," said Alla, "Has this been going on?"

Piney looked up at the sky and he moved his lips.

"Thirty-seven years," he said finally.

"How in the name of God did it start?" said Alla.

"Truth to tell," said Piney, "I don't remember. But it must have been something."

"Oh," said Alla, "I wonder."

"Look," said Piney, "A good enemy is a lot more useful than a good friend. I can always count on Norris. He never wants to borrow money from me. He never wants me to fix his cat for nothing. All he wants to do is stomp the shit out of me. It keeps us alive. Hell, woman, I'm seventy-one. I'd a never made it this far without Norris."

Alla nodded. She got in the plane and she sat next to Pat in the back two seats. Du Pré got in beside Piney.

Piney started the engine and he turned the little plane around and he zigged and zagged through the rocks till he got to the runway and he punched the throttle and he took off.

They cleared a barbwire fence close to the end of the runway by three or four feet and Piney tilted the plane slightly to miss a tall cottonwood and he began to climb slowly to altitude. The engine ran perfectly. Piney's eyes flickered over the instrument panel and the horizon and the ground.

Du Pré relaxed. The man was good.

"One of these days," said Piney, "I think I'll break down and get a pilot's license."

"What was that?" said Alla. The cabin was noisy.

"I SAID ONE OF THESE DAYS I'M GOING TO GET A PILOT'S LICENSE," said Piney.

"I thought so," said Alla.

"Some people in Montana actually have them," said Pat Weller.

"Goddamned government interference," said Piney.

Du Pré laughed.

They flew for twenty minutes and came in over the huge heap-leach mine from the west. The mine was sprawled out and there were dozers working the spoil heaps and huge trucks carrying the pale ore from the big metal crushing mills to the leaching pads. Sprinklers on top of the ore piles distributed the cyanide solutions.

There was a big pond of used water at the base of the mine complex. It was brilliant turquoise.

"Those two buildings," said Weller, tapping Du Pré on the shoulder, "The white metal ones over there. They have 880 power lines, but there is no reason to have them there for anything but pumping. They're in the wrong place for anything else."

"There's the fissure," said Alla, "See that line headed east there?"

"I thought it was an underground stream," said Piney, "Hell, it runs straight over to Lodgepole. It's real odd. I don't know of another mark on the terrain like that."

"They hoped it would diffuse before it came out," said Alla, "It should have. Probably that's sealed off with bentonite, some accident or other. A fluke."

Du Pré looked down at the line snaking across the High Plains. It went straight, sometimes under low hills and on again. The hills were left by glaciers.

Du Pré looked ahead four or five miles and he saw the scar in the earth that was the little canyon where Billy Grouard and Danny Bouyer and the other young men had drummed and hid out from hard lives. The line ran to it and it stopped there.

"Things are so clear from up here," said Alla Weller.

"Yah," said Du Pré, "It is pret' straight line."

"If they pumped a lot of water, it could move through there in a matter of hours," said Pat Weller, "It would be damned unusual, but it could be. It very well could be."

"OK," said Du Pré, "How we prove that this is so? I can see it good but how do we prove that?"

"Oh," said Pat Weller, "We salt the injection well with something that is a radioactive marker, and when it comes out down here that will do it."

"How we get them to let us do that, put it in their well?" said Du Pré.

"I think we had better. . . . " said Pat Weller.

"No damned we," said Du Pré, "I slide in there, do it, you tell me how."

"I need to go back and see if they have any monitoring equipment that would pick up the tracer," said Pat Weller, "I expect they do. It is the one thing that someone who didn't like what they were doing could do to wreck their position. With this much money at stake, the people in charge are usually very clever."

"So if there is?" said Du Pré.

"Have to get it into the wellhead," said Pat Weller.

"Prolly don't have a lid that screws off," said Du Pré.

"No," said Pat Weller, "It's a bit more complicated than that."

"There's somebody down there!" said Piney. He tilted the plane and came around and over the open scar of the little canyon. There were six people in it, pulling things toward one wall of the canyon. A big drum and some blankets.

Du Pré looked down at Billy Grouard and his friends. They had sat still till the plane turned around.

Out there drumming. Not drinking the water.

Good kids.

That is the place, Du Pré thought, where Danny Bouyer die. Where he really die. End of his line for sure.

"Got to head back," said Piney.

"Thank God," said Alla.

"Alla," said Piney, "Don't you just love it up here?"

❧ CHAPTER 27 ❧

Jimmy was sitting on the little front porch of the house, looking sad. He was folding a piece of paper and unfolding it. A cigarette burned next to him, the tip out away from the flooring.

"Is Jeanne inside?" said Madelaine.

Jimmy shook his head.

"She is at the bar," he said, "She's been there since it opened. Mickey went to see a friend of hers. Jeanne hit her last night."

Du Pré waited by the cruiser.

Sometimes on the res, he thought, it's a bad winter all year long.

"We go down there, Du Pré," said Madelaine.

Du Pré nodded and he got in the cruiser.

"I am sorry," said Madelaine.

"She is pret' sick," said Du Pré, "You are trying to help her. I love you. It is all right. Maybe I let you talk to her there, I go out and see if that Billy Grouard is maybe at the little canyon."

"Yah," said Madelaine, "Jeanne is not going to be easy to talk to, yeah, you go do that. If I have to I call that Redfield."

Du Pré dropped her off and he drove on out of town

toward the little canyon where he had seen Billy Grouard and his friends the day before. From the air, as they tried to hide the drum.

He found the turnoff and he bumped along the rutted track to a place he could turn around. He shut the engine off and he got out and walked over to the place where the path that went down into the earth began. He looked at the bare earth. Lots of feet on it, all headed out. Maybe no one there at all.

Du Pré took short steps and he danced down the path to the bottom. It was steep but the footing was good. It hadn't rained in a while. Someone had dropped a cheap wind-breaker over a bush at the bottom. The jacket was torn at one shoulder, the sleeve ripped part away.

Du Pré walked toward the poison spring. He stopped by the little stream of water. There was a slight tinge of green on the stones near the surface. Algae was growing.

Du Pré saw a little flash of movement at about eye height off through the alders. He stopped and stared and waited for whoever it was to move again.

Another flash, through the branches and leaves. Du Pré heard a cough.

Du Pré rolled a smoke and he lit it and then he walked back a little and he took the path that went to the cave where Billy and his friends stored the drum and their few things.

Billy Grouard was sitting on a rotten log by the cave entrance. He looked up when Du Pré stepped out of the bushes.

"Yo," said Billy.

Television, Du Pré thought, reach damn everywhere. What I say? You Dude? Jesus.

"I fly over you yesterday," said Du Pré, "You guys all run, huh?"

"Cops are after Jesse," said Billy, "We thought maybe it was them."

"What Jesse do?"

"Steal some stuff from the grocery. Run out with it."

"He hungry?" said Du Pré.

"I guess," said Billy. He stood up. He was favoring his right foot.

"You sprain an ankle?" said Du Pré.

"Dropped a knife on my foot," said Billy, "But it isn't healing. Just stays open. Don't seem infected."

Du Pré nodded.

"That water was poison," said Du Pré.

Billy nodded.

"That mine is pumping stuff down into the ground and it came up here," said Du Pré, "You don't drink that water, do you?"

"No," said Billy, "Couple of the other guys do though."

"Danny drank a lot of it," said Du Pré.

"I guess," said Billy, "That Joe and Henry they came here a couple hours ago looking for Jesse, they laugh at me some and go. They are like some comedy act."

Du Pré nodded. A lot of cops were like that. They had to laugh or be carried away screaming.

"My foot hurts," said Billy, "You maybe give me a ride home?"

"Sure," said Du Pré.

Du Pré turned and he walked up the path. Billy hobbled along behind and he stopped frequently. His foot was hurting him a lot.

Du Pré waited at his car till Billy struggled up the path and got up over the lip and dragged the last few steps to the old cruiser. He got in, blenched.

"Maybe I take you to the doctor?" said Du Pré.

"Yah," said Billy Grouard, "My foot don't work so good, can't play no basketball, much."

He looked at the floor of the car.

"How does that mine get poison all the way over here?" he said, "They pump it into the ground?"

"Inject it," said Du Pré.

"So it kills Danny," said Billy Grouard, "Lots of babies are born crippled."

"Yah," said Du Pré.

"Somebody should kill them," said Billy.

Du Pré drove off and he turned on to the road and drove on in to the hospital. Billy got out and he went on in and he didn't say anything or look back.

Du Pré drove to the bar and he got out and went in. Jeanne and Madelaine were sitting in the corner. Jeanne had been crying. She had a drink in front of her and a plate with part of a cheeseburger and some french fries on it. She hadn't eaten much of it.

Du Pré pulled up a chair.

"Du Pré," said Jeanne, "That Bart waste his money some, eh?"

"He got a lot of money," said Du Pré, "Don't worry about that."

"I got such bad dreams," said Jeanne. "Sometimes when I am awake. Drink, they don't bother me for a couple hours maybe."

"She say Mickey is pregnant, too," said Madelaine.

"She kill me I tell you," said Jeanne.

Du Pré nodded. This was a family blowing completely apart.

"My boyfriend he is in jail," said Jeanne.

Du Pré nodded.

"What I do now?" said Jeanne.

"What you want to do?" said Du Pré.

"I want to go back to that hospital," said Jeanne, "I do better this time. But I bet Bart won't do that. Will he?"

"He do it," said Du Pré, "He was in those places dozens of times. Yeah, Bart do that for you. I ask him."

Jeanne started to cry.

Madelaine reached over and she held her.

The woman behind the bar looked on, her face sad. She came over.

"Jeanne," she said, "you'll be all right. Now, it wasn't too much longer I'd have had to tell you you can't come in here anyway."

Jeanne nodded.

"Your boyfriend picked fights. He can't come back at all, ever."

Jeanne nodded.

"You taking her somewhere?" said the woman.

"Yeah," said Madelaine, "We are. She maybe need another drink, though you don't mind."

The woman went and got one and brought it back. Madelaine gave her a five-dollar bill and she waved away the change.

"You want to go, talk to Mickey, maybe?" said Madelaine.

Jeanne shook her head.

"I call her, tell her we are taking you to a hospital," said Madelaine.

Jeanne nodded. Madelaine went off to the pay phone.

"My kids they are all fucked up, me," said Jeanne.

"They pretty good kids," said Du Pré.

"Where your kids?" said Jeanne.

"Jacqueline is in Toussaint, got her fourteen children," said Du Pré. "And Maria is in England, going to school."

"I ain't seen them ever," said Jeanne.

Du Pré didn't say anything.

Kept my mouth shut, better, thought Du Pré, she sure don't want to hear about other people's kids doing well.

Madelaine came back.

"Mickey is fine, she said," said Madelaine.

"Mickey can't talk," said Jeanne.

"Jimmy can," said Madelaine, "You know what I meant."

"I hit them both I think," said Jeanne.

"They are OK," said Madelaine, "They are happy you are getting help." Jeanne nodded.

Du Pré got up.

Du Pré bought a fifth of whiskey from the woman behind the bar.

"I hope she's OK," said the woman.

Du Pré nodded. He waited till Madelaine and Jeanne had gone out and then he followed.

✤ CHAPTER 28 ✤

A diesel dump truck with wheels ten feet high ground past Du Pré and Pat Weller. They were standing beside the roadway at the mine, and it was raining hard and steadily. Sometimes the rain turned to ice pellets. Du Pré tilted his head so his hat protected his face.

"Those damn trucks," said Weller, "They have four big electric motors, one in each wheel, runs off a diesel engine, like a railroad locomotive. Move a lot of rock, though."

"I wish you'd put on the hard hat, sir," said the flunky who was showing them around," It's company policy. If you won't, I'll have to ask you to leave."

Du Pré crumpled his old Stetson and he jammed it in his jacket's game pouch and he put on the white plastic hat. The ice pellets rang on it hard.

Flying over the mine Du Pré had no sense of the scale of the thing. Monstrous draglines and bulldozers with blades twenty feet wide chewed at the ore body. An entire mountain. The one next to it was being readied for mining. Blasting crews were removing the overburden of worthless rock. Been a perfectly good mountain.

"We can go through the crushing plant now," said the flunk. They trudged off to the gigantic metal building. The din from inside it was so loud Du Pré could feel the sound as well as hear it.

Pretty far from Pelon and his flute by the willows in the Sweetgrass Hills, Du Pré thought, Pret' far from the buffalo used to be here, when my people come down from Red River in the carts. You could hear them carts long way off, screek screek, hear them Métis fiddling. Never know that there was gold beneath the buffalo, the grass, the hills.

The flunk led them through a door and on to a catwalk. There were huge conveyors rattling. Dust everywhere. Men tiny in the scale of the plant walked here and there doing whatever.

Eating the mountain, Du Pré thought, the whole damn mountain. Leave piles of busted stone, leaking poison. I been to that Homestake Mine, the Black Hills, it is pret' bad there, too, but at least it is Pret' much underground. They are down below sea level there.

Them Sioux they bitch about it, but my people were in the Black Hills long time before them. Sitting Bull's grandfather Black Bull was the first Sioux to see them Black Hills. So the Sioux take them.

The flunk led them along the catwalk and they saw the broken rock being dumped in at the far end. Then the crushers ate it.

Damn big place.

The flunk led them back outside. Du Pré's ears rang.

"The concentrator is over here," said the flunk. He led them toward another building where the leached gold was extracted from the water. Vast tanks and an electric hum.

"Well," said the flunky, "How about a cup of coffee and a donut?" He was in his mid-twenties and obviously hated doing this.

"What are those two buildings over there," said Pat Weller. He pointed off toward the tops of the two white buildings at the base of the impoundment.

"Assaying equipment," said the flunky.

"Really?" said Pat Weller, "Well, as a mining engineer I must express amazement. Assaying equipment these days would fit in a large closet."

The flunky laughed uneasily.

"And why the power mainlines coming into it?" said Pat Weller.

"I don't know what to say," said the flunky.

"No shit," said Pat Weller, "Well, I just expect I'd like to have a look-see over there." He strode off through the mud toward the white buildings. Du Pré followed.

"The little shit'll have security on us in a minute," said Pat Weller, "But I damn well want to know if they are running. I'll bet they are. All this rain."

He started to run. Du Pré glanced back and he saw the flunky turn and begin to run toward a telephone booth standing out away from all of the noise of the crusher.

Weller loped along easily, not running hard but moving pretty fast. The mud was sticky and it clotted on their boot-soles. They dashed behind a couple down dump trucks and then down a path and across a catwalk that spanned an oozing seep that came through the earthen dam. The sound of the ore crusher was fading. The rain was coming down hard.

Pat Weller stopped by a small shack that had a sign on it warning of explosives stored within.

There was absolutely no one visible around either of the two buildings, which were larger than they had seemed at a distance.

They got up to the building and Weller pressed his ear against the steel wall.

A deep bass whine inside was gaining revolutions, somewhere something was whirling slowly and coming up to speed.

"Hot damn," said Weller, "We got to get up the side of the dam now."

He ran back toward the earthen dam that held in the unearthly turquoise waters of the settling pond. There was a path going up and it was slick with the rain. They struggled, sliding.

Du Pré looked off to his right. A four-wheel drive SUV with blue lights flashing was wallowing through the mud.

Pat Weller was wheezing with the effort. Du Pré caught up to him. Weller's face was pale and he looked sickly.

"Take these up there, pull the pins, and throw them out over the water," he wheezed. He handed Du Pré two short lengths of plastic pipe with penlight batteries taped to them. "The pins are here. You have seven seconds to toss them. The charges aren't large, but they'd hurt. Hurry!"

Du Pré took them and he started up the hill. He heard a siren behind him. The SUV was wallowing toward the dam face and Pat Weller.

It took Du Pré a long time to struggle up to the top of the

189

dam. There was no one on it yet but four men in blue hard hats were moving toward the end of the dam on his left. They weren't running but they were moving fast.

Down behind him a bullhorn sounded. The voice said to stop where they were.

Du Pré looked out over the water. He pulled one of the pieces of plastic pipe out and he pulled the pin and he flipped it out over the water. It exploded and Du Pré grabbed the other one and he did the same.

He turned and he started down the hill toward Weller. A couple of security guards were struggling up the slippery path. Du Pré got to Weller when they were still fifty feet away.

"Good," said Weller, "The tracers are spread. Now if they will just keep the pumps running here we'll have some hard evidence." His breathing was better and he had some color back.

Du Pré and Weller began to walk down toward the security guards. The guards stopped climbing and they waited.

"What the fuck are you *doing*?" said the older one, when they got down to them.

"Just curious, son," said Weller.

"Well," said the security guard, "You just curioused yourself into the damn jail. What did you toss in the pond."

"Me?" said Weller, "Why, nothing."

The guards looked at them. Then they went down the face of the dam. Du Pré and Weller followed and they got into the back seat of the SUV. The guard at the wheel waited until the doors shut and he turned the SUV around and he headed out toward the main gate.

The going was treacherous. The SUV was wallowing badly and the driver was gunning the engine too hard. Several times they almost foundered. It took twenty minutes for them to get to the security office.

A man in a damp suit was waiting there, along with the security chief, an old cop by the look of him.

"Weller," said the suit, "We gave you the courtesy of a tour. What the hell were you doing there?"

Weller just smiled at him.

"We could prosecute you," said the suit.

"Anything special you want to prosecute me for?" said Weller, "Quick, now, I do need to know."

"Trespass," said the suit.

"You invited us to take the tour," said Weller.

"You have to stay with the guide," said the suit. The flunky who had been shepherding them was off in a corner, looking sheepish.

"I'm sorry, Mr. Carmichael," said the flunk.

Carmichael ignored him.

"Get out," said Carmichael, "And we won't have you back on this property."

"Fair enough," said Weller.

"Who's this?" said Carmichael, staring at Du Pré.

"Friend," said Weller.

"Go now or we will prosecute," said Carmichael.

Weller shrugged. He and Du Pré went out to the old

cruiser they had come over in. They got in and Du Pré started the engine.

"I was thinking on letting you sneak in," said Weller, "But that was chancy, too."

"They maybe just shut down the pumps," said Du Pré.

"They can't do that," said Weller, "I alerted the State of Montana and the station is manned. So they have to get the pollution levels down. The isotope is dispersed. They can only tough it out now."

"Pret' simple," said Du Pré.

"I like simple things," said Weller, "Now, how about a drink."

❧ CHAPTER 29 ❧

Y ou sure you only got the fourteen?" said Du Pré. He was
at his daughter's house, which had been his and his parents' and the parents' of his father and his great-grandfa-
ther's, too. Du Pré and his son-in-law Raymond had added a
dormitory wing. Built a lot of bunk beds. Bart had given
Jacqueline and Raymond a commercial-grade washer/dryer
set. Jacqueline made firestarters from the lint and paraffin.
She sold thousands of them to stores to sell to tourists.

"I have my nuts tied off," said Raymond, "I say, look,
Jacqueline, it is enough. Fourteen is plenty children. I think
she agree. She have another couple babies, she did not, but at
least, me, I tried."

Du Pré laughed. His grandchildren were tearing around
the yard and the meadow, quarreling and taking care of each
other.

"You got so many they wear themselves out, each
other," said Du Pré.

"I got eight daughters," said Raymond, "To get married
off. That is a lot of guys march them up the aisle with my
rifle in their backs. I got six sons, I can bail out of jail, do
them father things. Don't you die on me, Du Pré, me I need
your help."

They were sitting out behind the house near one of the outbuildings that held the tools that four generations of Du Pré's had assembled. There was a complete sawmill in another building. A whole welding shop in another.

"Papa," said Jacqueline out the kitchen window, "You want mustard on your sandwich?"

"Yah," said Du Pré.

"Maybe I want mustard, too," said Raymond.

"You don't like mustard," said Jacqueline.

"Shut up," said Du Pré, "You are digging a hole, yourself."

"I am just a man," said Raymond, "I live in a hole."

Du Pré nodded. These Métis women, fierce.

"Cattle business is getting good some," said Raymond, "I inspect six shippings last week. Only one problem. Calf don't belong, that rancher. He is embarrassed, load it up, take it to the owner. So I believe him."

"One time, a while, is OK," said Du Pré, "They move around in the mountains some times. You got three in a row, same place, then maybe you go sit and wait."

"I don't got time," said Raymond, "I have to ask you go sit and wait."

"OK," said Du Pré, "I know which guys do that, I know where to wait. Better you are here, fourteen kids, than I am."

"Me," said Raymond, "I would not threaten you, like that."

"Huh," said Du Pré.

Jacqueline came out of the house with plates of sandwiches and pickles and homemade potato strings and cole slaw. She had two cans of beer under her arm.

"Eat some," she said, setting the food down, "I never see my Papa so much now. What is it that you do now?"

"Trying to find out why Jeanne Bouyer's son, he die," said Du Pré.

"Poor Jeanne," said Jacqueline, "Madelaine tell me about her a little."

"Yah," said Du Pré, "It is tough for her. I think she feels very bad about her daughter, what has happened."

"Does she know if it was her drinking?" said Jacqueline.

Du Pré shrugged.

"They tell her it was not she still think it was," said Jacqueline. "She is at that hospital again?"

"Yah," said Du Pré, "She is there sixty days this time. Cost forty thousand dollars this time. Bart, he say money does not matter."

"Bart is a good man," said Jacqueline.

"He got a girlfriend," said Du Pré.

"Oh," said Jacqueline, "That Bart he need a good woman. What is she like?"

"I only meet her once," said Du Pré, "She is working out at the dig in the Sweetgrass Hills."

"Bart is very sweet like a big puppy," said Jacqueline, "He is pretty dumb like a puppy, too."

"Eh?" said Du Pré.

"He don't think he knows anything," said Jacqueline, "He is so shy. Big puppy. Always afraid he pee in the wrong place."

Du Pré roared.

"Well," he said, "What maybe you tell him, so he don't have this woman walk away?"

"Bart is so sweet," said Jacqueline, "She walk away she don't like puppies anyway, so what good is she to him?"

Du Pré looked at his healthy grandchildren running free in the grass and chasing the horses who the older kids rode bareback with a length of baling twine for a halter.

Over on the res some can't run, Du Pré thought, some can't look at a schoolbook make any sense of it. All they got to look forward to is sniffing glue, for Christ's sakes. Dying in the winter they pass out in the snow. Dumb Indians, oh, yes, but why are they?

"What you thinkin', Papa?" said Jacqueline. She had got herself a glass of iced tea and she was nibbling a little piece of yellow cheese.

Du Pré shrugged.

"You are plenty mad there a moment," said Jacqueline, "I see that look, over your face, like a bird across the sun. Little shadow. You are plenty mad."

"Me, I get mad I don't understand things," said Du Pré.

"Men always get mad they don't understand things," said Jacqueline, "It is the way you funny people you are. You men. Make a mistake, you can't figure how you did that, you get mad. Me, I yell at you you get mud on my kitchen floor you get mad at me since I say it should not be there. I still say it should not be there."

"OK," said Raymond, "I go and mop."

"We are married all these years I still think that there is

hope, Raymond," said Jacqueline, "You guys got two heads, think with the little one all the time, no wonder. Maybe you all ought to be in hospitals."

"You say all this before," said Du Pré, "Many times. Me, Raymond, we will not change much I guess."

"Yes you will," said Jacqueline, "But you still don't tell me why you are so mad."

"This mining company," said Du Pré, "They put all this poison in the water, I think that is what kill Danny Bouyer, make his sister Mickey deaf and dumb. Other kids on the res."

"They always did that," said Jacqueline, "I read in the cities poor kids, live in tenements, they eat the paint they are hungry, paint has lead in it. So they are made sick all their lives."

"Yah," said Du Pré.

"That Tally he is in the hospital, he have three surgery and more to go, fix him, is that from a mine?"

Du Pré nodded.

"It is that they are poor, Papa," said Jacqueline, "Poor people they don't got a voice here, you know."

Oh, yah, Du Pré thought, we poor Métis, we carry them furs for the Hudson's Bay Company, we fight their wars, die, we fight wars down here, scouts for the army, we die, we get a little land in Canada and the English fight with us, they don't like our water customs. Don't like us, we are not white. We fight them, lose, we some come down here. We are poor here. We are always poor.

Little Gabriel Dumont, the little general, he say he can

wipe out the English soldiers. He could, too. But poor Louis Riel, he have a vision and he say no, so we lose. Gabriel Dumont is buried in the Sweetgrass Hills, no marker, so the priests can't find it. He hate the priests, they betray Louis Riel so the English can hang him.

"But you are plenty mad, Papa," said Jacqueline, "You don't do something stupid, heh?"

Du Pré shook his head.

"Mining company is a lot of people," said Jacqueline, "The people who make them do these things are not even here, so you don't shoot no one."

Du Pré nodded.

"Guys work there are just guys, some Métis, too. Good jobs are not easy to find in Montana. They are raising their families," said Jacqueline.

"Yah," said Du Pré.

"Well," said Jacqueline, "I just worry, my Papa, he got a temper, you know, bad one."

Du Pré looked at her. My temper is not that bad, he thought. I am a good Montanan, I only kill people really need it.

"Nobody, the mine, really need it, Papa," said Jacqueline.

Du Pré laughed.

"There is nobody there needs it, Papa," said Jacqueline.

"OK," said Du Pré.

"It is like the mud on my kitchen floor, Raymond," said Jacqueline, "He think I don't notice because he don't notice.

It is always he is puzzled, don't know how I notice what he does not."

Du Pré looked at her.

"Madelaine she is worried, too," said Jacqueline.

Du Pré nodded.

"So you just got to not get too mad," said Jacqueline.

"Well," said Jacqueline, "You and Madelaine come eat dinner?"

"Sure," said Du Pré.

"You are a very smart man, Papa," said Jacqueline.

✤ CHAPTER 30 ✤

The rain was pounding down. Du Pré smelled the wet. The ground was soaked enough so that there were a lot of puddles on it. Usually rain was sucked down as it hit. The droughts could last for years and the soil parched. Montana, the high desert.

"We're knocking off," said Big Jim, "Can't wash the soil out in the rain."

They were standing next to the excavations in the Sweetgrass Hills. The crew was scurrying around putting tarps over equipment and the shafts which cut down through time to bedrock.

"Did I tell you that I got a formal letter informing me that I would be prosecuted for trespass if ever I am found on any property owned by Persephone?" said Pat Weller.

"I don't get one of those," said Du Pré.

"I don't think they know who you are," said Pat, "But Bart and I will have great fun at the stockholders' meeting with it. I urged him to buy some more Persephone stocks but he told me . . . something rude."

"They do anything about that radioactive stuff we put in the water?" said Du Pré.

"Do what?" said Pat Weller, "That diffuses so rapidly

they could have carted off the whole impoundment and it still would have been out in places they couldn't find."

"How's Piney like standing around the spring with a jar?" said Big Jim.

"Loves it," said Pat Weller, "Norris comes by every afternoon and they yell at each other. Norris's wife sends hot dinners. Piney's got a life-size papier-mâché statue of Norris he paid some kid to make and he keeps shooting at it while Norris is standing up on the rim. Friendship like that is a rare thing."

Du Pré snorted. "Yah," he said, "I know two guys like that, they come to this bar every Saturday, seven, they sit at stools each end of the bar. Each drink they have, they move over one stool. When their stools are next to each other they have one drink and then fight. Every Saturday."

"When I was in Wyoming right out of college," said Pat Weller, "I went to town every Saturday. I was a bright young geologist from Yale. I would sit out of range and watch the cowboys. They savor fights like snobs savor good wine."

"Damn," said Big Jim, "This rain is something. I ain't seen it come down like this in a long time."

"Persephone is not happy," said Pat Weller, "Their system can't handle this amount of rainwater. They'll flood out and the EPA is just waiting for them now. Their stock dropped alarmingly yesterday."

Me, thought Du Pré, I would like to take some pieces of Danny Bouyer their fucking stock meeting, yes. Take Mickey.

"Well," said Pat Weller, "I think I'd like to go get a pizza and take it to poor Piney. I hate to think of him getting rained on with nothing to do but shoot at a papier-mâché statue of Norris."

"Will that get there this quick?" said Big Jim.

"That's the imponderable," said Weller, "How quickly the water percolates through to that little spring. No way to know. It may never even make it. So many variables."

"I'm needed here," said Big Jim, "If you think of it, tell Piney I got a dog needs a tail transplant."

"Done," said Pat Weller.

He and Du Pré walked down the hill to where Du Pré's cruiser was parked. The old car was coated in mud. There were clear places on the windshield where the wipers had scraped but the rest of the glass was opaque.

"Montana mud," said Weller, "Gumbo. I have been out in the country and had a storm kick up and the mud turned to grease and there I would have to sit for a day or two till it dried out."

Du Pré nodded. He'd done the same thing many times.

They got in and Du Pré wallowed around and headed downhill toward the highway fifteen miles away. It was mostly downhill, and any time that Du Pré had to go uphill he raced the engine and got every bit of speed he could on the downslope. They slopped and slewed and once almost slid off.

When they got to the highway the cruiser shuddered as the mud flew off the tires and slapped into the body. It took miles before most of it wore off.

The mud on the track going out to the little canyon where Piney was was so bad they had to abandon the car and walk, slogging slowly while the mud built up inches thick on their bootsoles.

There were two four-wheel drive wagons parked at the end of the track. Du Pré went to the spot where the path wound down the side of the canyon. It was wet and treacherous.

"This is not good," he said.

"At all," said Pat Weller. "Let me show you a trick, though." He took a very heavy plastic bag out of his backpack and he cut holes for his legs and he bagged himself and he handed one to Du Pré, who shrugged and did the same.

Weller held the bag bunched to his chest.

He sat carefully on the slick rock at the trail's edge. He slid off and he shot down the winding trail on his ass, throwing up yellow muddy water.

Du Pré laughed and he followed.

They stripped off the bags. There was a little mud on their pants but not much.

"I used to do that to get back down from mountains I was mapping," said Pat Weller, "We used to have races. Another geologist was killed, actually, missed a turn and went off a cliff. We were young then."

They went up the trail toward the spring.

They passed Norris's effigy. Someone had doused it in gasoline and set it alight and the papier-mâché was blackened and parts of the armature showed through.

There was a bright red tent at the little spring. Much of the brush had been cleared away. There was laughter coming from the tent.

Du Pré looked in, and he saw Piney and Norris. They were drinking from tin cups. They had cards on a blanket in front of them. They were drunk.

There was a lot of money in silver and bills on the blanket.

"We got company," said Norris.

"Shit," said Piney, "Catch us like this they won't know what to think. My leg's gone to sleep. I oughta get up, kick your ass but I can't."

"Afternoon, gentlemen," said Pat Weller.

"We are not," said Dr. Norris, "Goddamn gentlemen."

"Come on in," said Piney, "We just got a little game going."

Du Pré and Weller ducked and went on hands and knees into the tent. They turned and took their boots off and put them under the rain fly.

The tent was well-fitted, with sleeping bags and a cookstove and coolers and monitoring unit set up on a white plastic stand.

"Sensors in the spring," said Piney, "I expect when the isotope bleeds through it'll do it all at once."

Weller nodded.

"No telling when that will be, though," he said.

"Nope," said Piney. "You fellers play poker?"

"Sure," said Weller.

"Yah," said Du Pré.

"Sheep to the shearing," said Piney, "We're playing seven-card stud, two two two and pot."

"High stakes," said Weller.

"Christ," said Norris, "a wimp."

"Norris," said Piney, I would take you outside and kick the shit out of you but it's *too goddamn wet*."

"Pussy," said Norris.

"Say," said Piney, "Is it pretty muddy up there?"

"Yah," said Du Pré.

"Good," said Piney, "I got seven hundred of Norris's money and I need more and he can't leave till it dries out."

"He cheats," said Norris.

"We both cheat," said Piney, "I'm just better than you."

"Drink," said Norris. He jerked his head toward a case of half-gallons of bourbon. "Cups are there somewhere."

Du Pré got drinks for himself and Pat Weller.

It began to rain harder.

They played cards. Du Pré smoked from time to time. There was a vent at the top of the tent, and the blue tendrils curled up to it.

Piney won for a while, and then Du Pré.

Weller and Norris went down and down.

Du Pré was looking at his hole cards when the monitor began to crackle and then putter in a faster and faster rhythm.

"Well," said Piney, "It seems Persephone has decided to join us."

❖ CHAPTER 31 ❖

I don't know where he is," said Redfield, "He dropped out of school. Damned shame. Such a bright kid and now he's screwing up every chance that he had."

"You don't know where he is?" said Du Pré.

Redfield shook his head.

"I got the infection in his foot cleaned up and the wound closed," he said, "Billy was certain that it was pollution from the mine. It wasn't that, he had a pseudomonas infection. They are bastards, really resistant to antibiotics. He must have washed his foot with contaminated water. A lot of the streams around here have pseudomonas in them. It's pretty common."

"That spring out in their canyon, it was getting water directly from the mine," said Du Pré, "We put radioactive stuff in the water and it came up in the canyon."

"In what water?" said Redfield.

"In the pond at the mine," said Du Pré.

Redfield just shook his head.

"Persephone will just say that you ran a phony test—that you just contaminated the spring. They do that. It will take years in court and a lot of money, millions, and they will fight and delay every inch of the way."

Du Pré nodded.

"Joe and Henry might know where he is," said Redfield. "I have to go now. I have rounds to make."

They shook hands and Du Pré wandered out to the parking lot and he got in his cruiser and he drove down to the little Tribal Police Station.

The police cruiser parked in front had the windshield smashed, and the driver's window was starred.

Du Pré grinned. He went on in.

Henry was sitting at his desk, boots on top. He had a bandage on his forehead. He had a bandage on his right hand.

"Afternoon," said Du Pré, "How's Joe."

"Fuck you," said Joe from the back room, "in the goddamn ear." He came out carrying a Styrofoam cup of lousy coffee. He had a bandage on his left cheek and his right arm in a sling.

"This goddamned breed is laughing at us," said Henry.

"We're all goddamn breeds," said Joe, "I got white blood, so do you."

"My heart's pure Gros Ventré," said Henry, "You leave my grandpaw out of this."

"He thinks we're funny," said Joe, "He wants to know the story."

"Domestic disturbance," said Henry, "Cop's favorite. It's where we usually get killed. Bad guys, they don't want to kill us because everybody gets so mad. Wife and hubby and whatever, though, are so mad and so fucked up they don't care."

"So we go to this trailer house," said Joe, "and things are sailing out the windows and all and the walls are bulging on account of people being thrown against them, and we put on our best cop faces and we knock hard on the door."

"Then the door hit me," said Henry, "Big guy behind it. Takes it right off and it hits me. The guy, too. I go down."

"I rush inside waving my cop flashlight, the five-cell Rodney King special, there, and what do I find?" said Joe.

Du Pré shook his head.

"Whole fucking tribe in there. Domestic disturbance my ass, it was a fucking riot. They are tired of beating the shit out of each other so they all jump me. Whip my ass good, throw me out the door on top of Henry."

"Then the fuckers realize they are in trouble, so they stampede over us—we're out cold—and stomp us good. We lie there a while, sleeping peacefully. We wake up. It's so quiet. Some kind friend takes out the windshield of the car with an axe, we don't care, we're unconscious."

Du Pré howled.

"He thinks we're funny," said Henry.

"The Tribal Council is going to ask us rude questions and make fun of us, just trash our self-esteem," said Joe, "And all you can do is laugh."

Du Pré nodded.

"So I wake up and Joe wakes up and we flip a coin and we go to the hospital and here we are," said Henry.

"I'd arrest every one of those cocksuckers," said Joe, "But they all had their fucking faces painted and I don't even know who they are."

"But we done quelled that there domestic disturbance," said Henry, "It was real good police work."

"Yup," said Joe, "Without a single case of injury to any citizen. I know this for a fact because we were the only people in the emergency room."

"Now," said Henry, "what can we do for you, oh red brother?"

"I'm looking for Billy Grouard," said Du Pré.

"Christ," said Henry, "So are we."

Du Pré waited.

"He burgled a house," said Joe, "Somebody saw him leaving with a couple guns. Stole a little money and some cheap jewelry. I expect that he's in Billings, on the street."

"Maybe Great Falls," said Henry.

"Warrant out on him," said Joe.

Du Pré shook his head.

"We see too much of that," said Henry, "Good kid, doing great in school, suddenly, boom all to shit. I liked Billy. Still do. But there's enough lives in the toilet around here. Usually it's drugs gets them. I don't know what happened to Billy."

"What you want with Billy?" said Joe.

"Tell him we got evidence about the mine, poison the water," said Du Pré, "I thought maybe he like to know that."

"Oh," said Henry, "Your woman here looking after Mickey and Jimmy Bouyer? Mickey's pregnant I hear. Sweet kid, real pretty."

Du Pré nodded.

"What about the mine?" said Joe.

"They are leaking heavy metals into the water," said Du Pré, "It is probably why Mickey is deaf and she can't talk."

Joe nodded.

"Yeah," he said, "Like all them Navajo dying near that coal plant, or the uranium miners."

"You hear anything about Billy Grouard, you maybe let me know?" said Du Pré.

"He'll get picked up," said Henry, "We'll let you know."

The radio began to squawk. Then the telephone rang. Henry picked it up.

Henry's boots hit the floor. He put one hand on his forehead.

"Yeah," he said. "We will." He hung up.

"Billy Grouard just shot two guys at the mine," said Henry, "One is dead. One probably will die."

"Where's Billy?" said Du Pré.

"In one of the buildings out there," said Henry, "He's wounded."

"Shit," said Du Pré.

"Yeah, shit," said Joe, "Off the res, not our jurisdiction. But if he gets away, comes back here . . . "

"We get to shoot him," said Henry, "We're the good guys. I read that."

"I go out there," said Du Pré.

Henry nodded.

"They'll be happy to see you," said Joe, "We heard about you and the guy . . . Weller? . . . don't be a dumbass, you look Indian, somebody'll shoot you."

Du Pré sighed.

210

"Well," said Henry, "I forgot to tell you, Joe, they want us to come on out. Seems that Billy will talk with us."

"Oh, good," said Joe.

"You want to come, Du Pré?" said Henry.

"Yah," said Du Pré.

"We can take his car," said Joe, "It's got a windshield."

"What a good idea," said Henry, "I forgot ours doesn't."

"It doesn't," said Henry, "I looked again, hour ago, it was still gone, just not there."

"OK by you, red brother Du Pré?" said Joe.

Du Pré nodded.

"We need guns?" said Henry.

"No," said Joe, "Every asshole with a badge will be there with a gun, want to use it. They think. I did once. I don't like to think about it."

"You ever kill anyone, Du Pré?" said Henry.

Du Pré nodded.

"Yeah," said Henry.

They walked out to Du Pré's old cruiser and they got in and Du Pré drove off toward the mine.

"Anybody want a stick of chewing gum?" said Joe.

Du Pré shook his head. He was rolling a cigarette.

"Nah," said Henry.

"Good," said Joe, "I only got the one and I would have hated telling you folks there wasn't enough."

✤ CHAPTER 32 ✤

Du Pré and Henry and Joe were standing a little ways
away from a crowd of workers who were talking
angrily among themselves. The mine manager was chewing
on a toothpick and he had mud all over his low shoes. Three
sheriff's cars were parked in a row, lights flashing, the
deputies hunkered behind them in bulletproof vests.

The deputies all had assault rifles.

"This is terrible," said the mine manager.

"Yah," said Du Pré, "blow your production all to hell."

The mine manager didn't hear him.

"So he's in that machine shed," said Henry.

"Billy Grouard's Last Stand," said Joe, "Which one of us
got shot the last time?"

"I did," said Henry.

"If you mean the *one* shotgun pellet the woman you were
boning last April got into you, or her husband did, it don't
count," said Joe.

"It was two shotgun pellets and I could have been
killed," said Henry.

"Nicks you get in your endless hunt for pussy *don't count*,"
said Joe.

"Are these guys for real?" said the mine manager to Du

Pré, "That bastard in there killed two of our employees and they *joke?*"

"Yah," said Du Pré, "They are like that."

"What are you going to do?" said the manager.

"I am going to wait a while," said Du Pré, "Then see what Joe and Henry they are doing. Maybe I go talk to Billy."

"Phone!" yelled the flunk to the mine manager. The manager went over to the security truck.

"We were thinking," said Joe, looking at Du Pré, "That we might ask you to flip a coin. We each cheat a lot and that way there wouldn't be any hard feelings."

Du Pré nodded. He dug a quarter out of his pocket.

"Heads, tails," said Du Pré, pointing at Joe and then Henry, "Tails wins."

Du Pré flipped the coin and he caught it and slapped it on the back of his hand. He looked at it.

"Me, I go," he said, "It landed on the edge first."

"Them Métis is dumb fucks," said Henry, "You can count on 'em."

"What you do maybe is see that them deputies don't shoot us both we come out," said Du Pré.

"Oh, good," said Joe, "We get to *assist.*"

The mine manager came back.

"The media is on the way," he said. He looked miserable.

"You been lying to them a long time," said Du Pré, "It will be all right."

"What do you mean?" said the mine manager.

"Good luck," said Joe.

Du Pré strolled over to the single door next to the huge

overheads. He knocked a couple times and then he opened it and he stood in the light of the doorway.

"Hey, Billy," he yelled, "It is Du Pré. I am going to come in, talk. I don't got no gun."

Du Pré waited.

"Yah," said Billy Grouard, "You come."

Du Pré went in. He shut the door behind him.

"I am over here," said Billy.

Du Pré peered at the dark machinery, the dump trucks and the dozers and smaller vehicles at the mechanics' stands.

Billy Grouard was sitting in a folding chair by a workbench.

Du Pré walked over to him.

"I am thirsty," said Billy.

Du Pré looked at the blood soaking Billy's shirt and right pants leg. He'd taken a slug in the gut, low down.

"I get you some water," said Du Pré. He walked past Billy and he found a cooler with a five-gallon carboy of water upended in it. He lifted the water jug out and turned it over and set it down. The cooler was plugged into a socket on the floor. Du Pré unplugged it. He stuck the cord in the top bin and he dragged the whole thing over by Billy and he went back and got the jug and put it back in. Billy looked at him, his face pale.

Du Pré handed hin several cups of water, the little cones that hold only a couple swallows.

"What you want to do?" said Du Pré.

"I shoot myself, a minute," said Billy.

Du Pré nodded.

"Look," said Billy, "My life is ended here, now, I don't got to rot in that Deer Lodge Prison."

Du Pré nodded. "Don't got to do that, Billy."

"I lie to you," said Billy, "I drink a lot of that water from that spring. We call it our sacred water. Carry bottles of it home."

"I am sorry," said Du Pré.

Billy shrugged.

"You tell my people I do this for them?" said Billy.

Du Pré nodded.

"Maybe you make a song for me, eh, Du Pré?"

"Yah," said Du Pré, "I do that."

"Good," said Billy Grouard. "Me, I am afraid but I guess you going to do this you got to do it quick when you do it."

"Trial would help your people," said Du Pré, "Raise a big stink, you know. You do that. Trial don't work out, you kill yourself later."

Billy looked off toward a line of light that shot under one of the big overhead doors that didn't quite come down all the way.

"Thanks," he said, "I think I do that. But, now, can I get out of here and not get shot?"

"Sure," said Du Pré, "I carry you out. I don't think you can walk."

"Hah," said Billy, "I am too big. There is a cart over there. I can sit on it."

Du Pré looked at a tool cart over by the workbench. Big rubber wheels on it. Probably get over the dirt and ruts.

"OK," said Du Pré, "Where is that gun?"

215

"Here," said Billy. He reached down and picked up a cheap bolt-action .22 and he handed it to Du Pré. Du Pré took the bolt out.

"Well," said Du Pré, "We maybe go now."

Billy began to sing in a tongue Du Pré didn't know.

Kid probably singing his death song, Du Pré thought, or wants to and don't know how. Sounds like a movie death song.

Billy quit.

Du Pré sighed. Death songs were a lot longer.

He went to the cart and he dumped the tools off it and he pulled it over to Billy and he helped him on to it. Billy slumped against the steel siding. He held his hands on his gut.

Du Pré pulled the cart over to the door, he opened it and he tugged the cart over the threshold and he blinked hard at the light.

The deputies were standing up behind their cars, rifles pointed to the sky.

"He need a medic," Du Pré said.

Two EMTs pushing a gurney started over to where Billy and Du Pré were.

Joe and Henry limped to them.

"Billy," said Joe, "You better have a damn good explanation for this."

"Kiss my ass," said Billy.

Joe shrugged. A couple deputies were moving over behind the EMTs. They still had on their vests but they weren't carrying the rifles.

An ambulance wallowed over the rutted yard, lights blinking.

"Thanks," said one of the deputies to Du Pré.

Du Pré nodded. He stepped back and let the EMTs work on Billy. While they did that the deputy read Billy his rights.

The EMTs loaded Billy on to the gurney and the gurney in to the ambulance. The EMTs got in and so did the deputy. The ambulance wallowed back across the rutted yard and it turned toward the main gate.

"Poor little son-of-a-bitch," said Henry.

"Yah," said Du Pré.

"Thank you," said the mine manager, smiling at Du Pré.

"Kiss my ass," said Du Pré, "I don't do it for you shits. This is going to be, one big mess of trouble, you."

The manager scuttled off.

The workers were trickling away to their jobs.

Du Pré and Joe and Henry stood there while the mine came back to life.

"The one guy's gonna live I guess," said Henry, "Other one took a slug right through the old earhole."

Du Pré nodded.

"I take you back now," he said.

They walked to Du Pré's old cruiser and got in and Du Pré started the old car and they drove down to the main gate. The guard wasn't back to the little kiosk yet. They drove on.

Du Pré fished the whiskey out from under the seat and he had some.

Henry took it and he had some, and so did Joe.

"Pret' good," said Henry, "For a shit's day's work."

"Poor little fucker," said Joe.

"There is a lot of Billys," said Henry.

"Yah," said Du Pré.

"I liked Billy," said Henry.

"I write a song for him," said Du Pré.

CHAPTER 33

S o Billy guns down two ordinary schlunks doing their jobs for their hourly wage," said Bart. "Life makes me want to puke, time to time, you know. Poor everybody."

Du Pré nodded. They were sitting at a picnic table near the dig. The moonsuited students were washing out soil samples on the screen tables. Big Jim Lascaux was down in one of the holes peering at a fireline, the black charcoal stratum where old campfires had sat.

Gretchen Kidder rubbed Bart's shoulder.

"Look, big guy," she said, "You can't fix everything. I know you want to, but you just can't."

"He don't want to get off," said Du Pré, "that Billy, he say he will go through the trial, get Persephone, then kill himself."

"Jesus," said Bart, "that poor kid."

"Yah," said Du Pré, "But he know what he is doing. You know, he was a good basketball player, but that poison water rob him of that. Like it rob Danny Bouyer. Good students, but their minds are not so good anymore. Can't concentrate. So he knows what he is doing there."

"It's no different from the tobacco companies," said

Gretchen Kidder, "The evidence that they deal death is overwhelming, but they have enough money to keep going."

"The difference is that people *choose* to smoke," said Bart.

"Four hundred thousand deaths a year in this country and you want to quibble," said Gretchen, "I'm talking about what big money and big business *does*. Obviously, we the people of the United States let them do it."

"Jeanne will be back tomorrow," said Bart, "Short stay this time. I hope this one takes. Yeah, hell, she goes off on a toot again I'll send her back. God knows I did dozens of times before I quit."

"Why did you quit?" said Gretchen.

"I don't know," said Bart, "Character had nothing to do with it. I just quit."

Du Pré laughed. He remembered Bart's bloated red face in the window of the gross house that Bart later burned down, cursing at Du Pré. Long time ago.

Du Pré rolled a cigarette.

"I like them tobacco companies," he said.

Gretchen laughed.

"I like them whiskey companies," said Du Pré, "People around here they make whiskey but it is pret' bad."

"Well," said Gretchen, "The world goes on from one fool disaster to another, as always. Come on now, I want to show you what we've found."

She got up, tall and graceful. She had a long, kind face and very shrewd blue eyes.

Bart and Gretchen walked hand in hand, and Du Pré followed. She led them to some big white wall tents and inside.

The air was warm and smelled of cloth and wax and the sun's heat. There were several trestle tables set up and hundreds of stone tools, each marked with a small white blot on which a filing number had been put in black ink.

"These are very old," said Gretchen. She held up a scraper, a big chunk of gray-yellow chert crudely bashed on one side.

"Nothing like the Folsom points," she said. "These people weren't very good at knapping tools. But the stuff got the job done. Look at these knives . . . "

Du Pré held one of the black blades. They were obsidian flakes three inches or so long and an inch wide.

"They may have been mounted in a wooden handle," said Gretchen, "Which long since rotted away."

"How old are these?" said Bart.

"Perhaps twelve thousand years," said Gretchen, "The tests aren't done yet. They take a while, and have to be done in stages."

Long time gone, Du Pré thought, I wonder what these people were like? Pretty much like we are. Without no CD players.

"All this from a summer?" said Bart.

"Perhaps three times this," said Gretchen, "This is an incredibly rich site. We've already shipped three tons of specimens this year. Some we find with the cracked bones of bison, mammoths, what have you. This spot was a prime campsite for thousands of years."

"When are they going to start on the other one?" said Bart.

"What other one?" said Gretchen.

"The one Benetsee pointed out to Big Jim," said Bart.

"Maybe never," said Gretchen, "It's owned by the people of the United States, so the Bureau of Land Management has it. They may never grant permission."

"Jesus Christ," said Bart, "They'll grant permission to grind all these hills up into scouring powder, but they won't allow an archaeology team to dig?"

"The Indian activists claim that hair is burial material, sacred material," said Gretchen, "Which merely means that they want to control it. So, the BLM dithers. That's how it is. This is private land we are on here, and archaeology only goes on on private lands in this country now."

"I'll buy it," said Bart.

"From the BLM?" said Gretchen, "Impossible."

"I'll buy something they really want and trade 'em off," said Bart, "Now if you'll excuse me I got to go and call Lawyer Foote."

Bart went out of the tent.

"He's such a pussycat," said Gretchen, "I don't think I've seen him angry before."

Du Pré grunted.

"Well," said Gretchen, "I suppose we could go look down on Big Jim as he stands in water up to his neck picking at some old charcoal."

They walked down to the lowest of the dig sites and they leaned over and looked.

Big Jim and an assistant were digging at the fireline with dental tools. They would pick and pick and then take some

222

tiny fragment out and put it in a tiny plastic bag and label it and tuck it in a pocket.

"Ho," said Du Pré, "What are you finding?"

"Bird bones," said Big Jim, "Ducks, I think."

"Bart he is going to go and buy that place that Benetsee pointed out to you," said Du Pré.

"Good," said Big Jim, "If I have to deal with those BLM assholes I'll be up on murder charges. First degree. I will have thought about it before I did it."

"You are thinking about it now," said Du Pré.

"You don't know 'em," said Big Jim, "Like I do."

"You could come up out of there," said Gretchen, "and leave that to the peons like me. I only have a bachelor's degree."

"I kinda like it down here in my hole," said Big Jim, "I can't see the twentieth century from it. It's a good hole and I feel comfortable down here. Nice deposits. It soothes me. Why, tens of thousands of years from now when that fucking mess at Big Sky is excavated and archaeologists are puzzling over what will doubtless be known as The Bad Taste Culture I won't be here. But they will."

"Come up anyway," said Gretchen, "and have a coffee and talk to Du Pré and Bart. Come on."

Big Jim looked up. He sighed. He squelched over to the ladder and he grabbed the two-by-fours nailed crossways for steps and he hauled his huge body up. He stepped out away from the bars. He was wearing hip boots which hadn't been quite tall enough.

Big Jim laid down on his back and he lifted his legs to

empty the water and break the suction and then he pulled the hippers off and he stood there leaking on to the churned earth and grass. A cold wind had come up but Big Jim ignored it. He went to the picnic table and he sat down and he fished a cigarette out of his pocket and he lit it and he smoked and looked off in the direction of the site that Benetsee had pointed out.

"I don't know how to tell Bart," said Big Jim, "My heart just sank the day that that old fart pointed that out. I knew we'd probably never get to dig there. Damn, maybe the most important site in North America and it would sit there."

Bart wandered back.

"Somehow," he said, "I'll get that."

Big Jim nodded.

"What tribe is Benetsee?" he said.

"Don't know," said Du Pré.

"How old is he?"

Du Pré shook his head.

"I'd like to carbon-date his goddamn hair," said Big Jim.

"How does he know that there was an old camp there?" said Gretchen.

"The songs," said Du Pré.

"Songs?"

"The old songs," said Du Pré, "They maybe last longer than that damn hair you are digging up."

"Oh," said Gretchen.

❦ CHAPTER 34 ❦

"I am in the sweatlodge and I am told, play the Stick Game, take care of your children, live, the past let us keep for you," said Jeanne, "So I get out and I get dry and I tell my counselor what I heard and that I better go home and she say yes. So I am here."

Madelaine and Du Pré were sitting in the front seat of Du Pré's cruiser and Jeanne was in the back. She was drinking a lot of pop.

"Last time you seem to be beaten up," said Madelaine, "I think you do better this time."

"I don't know that my team, they will want me back," said Jeanne.

"You got some power they will," said Madelaine, "Anyway what team? There are what a dozen women play on that team. They don't go, every pow-wow, every time. They got lives you know, troubles, good things."

"I did not mean to do bad to Danny and Mickey and Jimmy," said Jeanne "But I did and now I got to go on, do better for them."

"Sure," said Madelaine.

Du Pré glanced off at a big porcupine waddling through a pasture. Long way from food and a tree to hide in. But he know where he is going. Porcupines, they dance funny, Du Pré thought, rattle them quills. They are really stupid. Been here longer than just about anything, being stupid. I got to remember that smart don't help some times, long times.

"Hey Du Pré," said Jeanne, "You can have some whiskey it don't bother me any, you are being nice though and I thank you."

"You sure?" said Du Pré.

"Yah," said Jeanne, "I am sure. Me, I am sure about a lot of things."

Du Pré fished the whiskey out from under the seat and he had some. He hated driving long distances. He didn't mind so much if he was a little drunk. Not a lot. Kept him from being bored.

"OK," said Du Pré, tipping the bottle, "You want a smoke?"

"Sure," said Jeanne.

Du Pré rolled her a cigarette with his right hand. He licked the paper and he handed it to Madelaine.

When they got to Lodgepole they went directly to Jeanne's little house. Jimmy and Mickey were standing out front, dancing, when the car pulled up. They ran over.

Jeanne struggled out and she held her children and they all cried.

Du Pré and Madelaine sat in the car for a while. Finally Madelaine leaned out of the window and she tugged on Jeanne's long blouse.

"We are going, the bar, get something to eat and then

home," she said, "You come there if you want. You all come there."

Jeanne shook her head.

"I call you, I thank you," she said.

"You let me know the next Stick Game," said Madelaine, "I bet on you."

Jeanne laughed. Du Pré let the engine rev up and then he let it drop and he put it into drive. The transmission clunked some.

I only got two hundred thousand miles maybe on this, can't get my money's worth any more, Du Pré thought, that damn transmission she will seize up you bet probably on the way home.

He stopped at a gas station and he checked the transmission fluid. Low. He added two quarts. Uh-oh.

"What is wrong, Du Pré," said Madelaine, "Your horse here gonna throw a shoe maybe?"

Du Pré shrugged.

They took off and the transmission sounded fine. Du Pré kept an ear cocked for nasty noises. Nothing.

He got the cruiser up to eighty and they shot along to Malta and Du Pré stopped at a bar that had good hamburgers. They went in and ate and played one game of pool.

Madelaine always beat him.

She never seemed to be winning until she would run the last two or three balls and the eight.

Du Pré handed over the usual five dollars. Madelaine paid for the hamburgers with it.

They went on. The air was dusty and the sun was sinking and the west was toning in gold deeper by the minute, and would be red in an hour. The sun was shining right through the back window. Du Pré turned the rear-viewmirror so it wouldn't flash in his eyes when he dipped over a hill.

"That Jeanne be all right this time," said Madelaine, "I think she will."

Du Pré nodded.

"It is very hard," she said, to do what she got to."

"Yah," said Du Pré.

"What is Bart going to do about Billy Grouard?" said Madelaine.

Du Pré shrugged and the transmission screamed and then there was a heavy thump and the car jumped sideways and Du Pré leaned against the wheel and he turned it to keep it on the road. He hit the brakes.

There were no brakes.

The engine was racing.

Du Pré grabbed the hand brake and he pulled. It came out of the tube that held it.

They rolled downhill at eighty. Up a long grade, slowing. Du Pré couldn't turn the engine off because the steering column would lock the front wheels.

The engine blew. A piston shot through the hood. Radiator fluid covered the windshield.

Du Pré stuck his head out the window. They had a hundred yards to go to the top of the hill. The car was slowing, but they were still going fifty miles an hour.

They crested the hill. Du Pré looked ahead. There was a

tractor hauling a lowboy trailer filled with huge round hay bales, one ton each.

There was a semi coming up the other lane.

Du Pré cursed and he rolled around the trailer and the tractor and the driver of the semi blinked his lights on and off. Du Pré waved his arm frantically. The semi braked.

Du Pré ducked in front of the tractor with thirty feet to spare.

The downgrade was long and winding and it wound up at the bottom on a tight right-hand turn followed by a couple of hairpins.

Du Pré cursed.

They shot downhill.

He saw a stock tank over on the left side of the road, perhaps an acre of pond.

"You put on the seat belt," he yelled at Madelaine. She fumbled with the seat. The belt was wedged down between the cushions.

Du Pré took a hard left and he shot across the little barrow pit and the car lurched once and hit a barbwire fence which twanged like a banjo string. The right front tire blew.

They bounced across the field and hit the water and they were both thrown against the dashboard but not too hard. The car almost made it to the other side before it stopped. The mud covered everything, including Madelaine and Du Pré.

The water was only two feet deep.

Du Pré mopped at his face with a greasy towel that lived on the floor of the cruiser. He could see.

"Hey, Du Pré," Madelaine laughed, "That was some fun

yes! I am paying two dollars that ride at a carnival! Hah! We have good luck!"

"Shit," said Du Pré. He got out and he squelched back to the rear of the cruiser. The trunk had popped open. He looked in. His fiddle was there, it had bounced around some but the case wasn't scratched. He picked it up and he pulled a jeep bag out and threw it on the roof. A sack with some food and candles. A first aid kit.

The semi had backed up and the driver was running across the field to the cruiser.

Madelaine was laughing.

"Everybody all right?" said the trucker.

"Yah," said Du Pré, "I am sorry, my transmission blow."

"It come clean off," said the trucker, I saw it still flying when I got to the hilltop. You're lucky. Cut your brake lines when it went?"

"Yah," said Du Pré.

"I radioed for help," said the trucker, "I'll call 'em back and tell 'em everybody is OK."

Du Pré nodded. He was pulling things from the trunk and tossing them to Madelaine.

She piled them on the grass past the torn-up black earth where the cattle had cut the earth getting water.

"The cooler and my jacket in the back seat," said Madelaine, "Also you better get your whiskey. Stuff from the glove box. I don't think your cruiser drive away from this one."

"It is dead," said Du Pré.

A light plane flew over low, probably the rancher who

owned the stock tank. The plane turned around and made another pass.

Du Pré sat on the duffel and he had some whiskey and he rolled a smoke. The water hadn't hit his shirt pocket. His shepherd's lighter worked fine.

"Pret' funny," said Madelaine, "Better tell them Sheriff I am driving."

Du Pré looked at his whiskey. He nodded.

Madelaine sat next to him. She laughed and laughed.

"When your car die it die," she said.

Du Pré nodded. He smoked.

"Play me some song, Du Pré," said Madelaine.

Du Pré opened his fiddle case. The fiddle was fine.

He rosined the bow and he tuned the fiddle.

He played.

"I never heard you play that before, Du Pré," said Madelaine.

"I just think of it," said Du Pré, "It is for that Billy Grouard."

Madelaine hugged him.

They waited.

❖ CHAPTER 35 ❖

I'll find you some old piece of cop shit had the back seat puked on so often it's pinto," said Bart, "But for now you'll just have to look like some rich cocksucker from California."

Du Pré looked at the expensive Land Rover. He curled his lip. He spat in the dirt.

"Me, I have to go play at this festival us poor Métis are putting on and I got to drive some rich guy's car," said Du Pré, "The other Métis they will make fun of me and try to borrow money, gamble with it."

"OK," said Bart, "How about I buy you some ragass old pickup truck?"

"It, the old truck, would have more class," said Du Pré, "You know I drove one of your Land Rovers a while there and real estate agents they began to follow me, bankers, them too."

"I am going to buy three or four old pieces of cheap cop shit," said Bart, "So I am not embarrassed like this again."

"Well," said Du Pré, "I am not an ungrateful man, you are one of my best friends but you got no class. I mean, soon as that Mercedes-Benz they make some four-wheel drive thing you buy that. Rolls-Royce. Maybe you have that Ferrari make you up one special. Put a skunk tail on the radio antenna."

"OK," said Bart, "I apologize for fucking breathing."

"That don't take no Ferrari," said Du Pré, "I quit picking on you now."

"Good thing," said Madelaine, "I am about to tear your head off, Du Pré, why you so mean to Bart, here?"

"I worry him I don't do this," said Du Pré.

"It's true," said Bart, "I live on the contempt of Booger Tom and Du Pré. Without them despising me I don't know who I am."

"OK," said Madelaine, "So we are going all the damn way to Lewistown for this festival, yes, and Tally he will be there?"

"Yes," said Bart, "He's in good shape, too. Seven surgeries later. But the wound is clean and closed. Poor guy. He lived with that for over thirty years."

"It never heal?" said Du Pré.

"It would close over time to time," said Bart, "But always it would flare back up. Chronic infection."

"I'm going to pick up Gretchen," said Bart, "So you can take this one and I'll take the other one."

"You got three of them," said Du Pré, "Who is driving the third?"

"Booger Tom," said Bart, "Is using it on the ranch till his old pickup is fixed."

"He will wreck it," said Du Pré.

"I expect so," said Bart, "But not until his pickup is fixed. What he'll do, probably, is stable a goat in the Rover that will eat all the upholstery and shit all over everything."

Du Pré started to pile the luggage that Madelaine and he were taking to the festival in the back of the Rover. He put his fiddle case on the back seat. He put the two coolers there, too.

"Well," said Bart, "I'll see you." He got in the green Rover and he drove slowly off.

"Well," said Du Pré, "I will maybe not pick on Bart so much you think I should not."

"You guys, you never quit till you draw blood," said Madelaine, "Now Gretchen she have to listen to Bart whine about how mean you are to him, while she think, OK, why don't you just punch that Du Pré, put his lights out, eh?"

"I don't think Gretchen think that," said Du Pré, "She is pretty nice lady."

"We been listening to guys whine for maybe a million years before money is even invented," said Madelaine, "Don't be telling me this bullshit just start when they invent money. I know how women think, Du Pré, you guys never figure it out."

They got in and drove off and Du Pré got out to the highway and he pushed the Rover up to seventy and that was as fast as it drove without the wheels shaking.

They drove for twenty miles.

Du Pré looked in the rearview mirror. He saw an old car coming up behind him very fast. A Plymouth, too. White. Old cop car.

The Plymouth flashed past doing a hundred and ten or so, Bart was grinning at Du Pré in the mirror and then he stuck his left arm out and he gave Du Pré the finger as he shot up the long grade ahead and out of sight.

"Ho," said Madelaine, "He piss in your Post Toasties, for sure."

"That fucker," said Du Pré, "He have that car all along."

"You have not heard the last of this," said Madelaine, "That Bart he with fight back now, not put up with you and that Booger Tom."

"Asshole," said Du Pré, "I got to poke along this English piece of shit while he is there right away."

"You are whining, Du Pré," said Madelaine, "your Post Toasties they are wet and don't smell good."

Du Pré grunted and he rolled a cigarette and he lit it and he smoked and then after he tossed the butt out he pulled the whiskey bottle from under the flip-up armrest and he had a drink.

"I just kill him, I think," said Du Pré, "He is going to embarrass me again, you know this is not over. I think maybe I want to go to Lewis town late tonight when it is dark."

"Whine, bitch, whine," said Madelaine, "Me, I am going to find that Gretchen when we get there and we are going to go and drink, say bad things about you guys."

"He has to pick her up," said Du Pré, "I am thinking maybe I can get there before he does."

"You don't think he think of that?" said Madelaine.

"Bart can be pretty stupid," said Du Pré.

"All damn weekend you guys, you will be putting scorpions in each other's boots," said Madelaine, "You bother me, either of you, die."

"It is war," said Du Pré.

"Guy thing," said Madelaine, "Women invent it though, get you silly assholes out of the house, so there is peace."

"Anything us guys invent?" said Du Pré.

Madelaine thought.

"Farts," she said, "You guys invent them. No other explanation. Lots of noise and it smell bad. Got no points otherwise. Guy stuff."

Du Pré had some more whiskey.

"Can't think of anything else," said Madelaine, "Farts the only thing for sure."

"Fucking Bart," said Du Pré.

"Bart stick it to you good," said Madelaine, "I am glad for him."

"Why he do that?" said Du Pré, "He knows how much I hate this Land Rover. That is why he do this."

"I don't listen to this all the fucking way, Lewistown," said Madelaine," You and Bart, you go off in the corner, play dead. I don't listen to this, all the way, Lewistown. I drop you off, you take the bus or something."

Du Pré had some more whiskey.

"How is that Jeanne?" said Du Pré.

"Oh, her," said Madelaine, "I almost forget her I am so fascinated, you and Bart. Jeanne, oh, yes, my cousin. She will be there, there is a Stick Game. Us Métis love to gamble."

"This pret' big festival for the first one," said Du Pré.

"Well," said Madelaine, "Us Métis we are everywhere and we stay out of sight, pret' much, the res. But here are a lot of us, you know."

"Lewistown on the Musselshell River," said Du Pré, "That is where my great-grandpa he come, 1886. Got a bunch of kids, cart, couple horse, shovel, hoe. They pick them mussels, sell them to people who make buttons."

"I got some of them buttons," said Madelaine, "My people do that too."

The buttons were mother-of-pearl, hand-picked shells.

Didn't have no money they come here, Du Pré thought, they come right down over there, where the road it goes south, hunt the buffalo in the fall. When the English defeat us, some of us come down here, to live, but we are not Indians, not Americans, no one knows that we are here. That Black Jack Pershing he round us up, 1911, put us in boxcars, send us to North Dakota, that Pembina.

Four hundred Métis they die on the trip or freeze to death after we get there. My grandmother she lose two sisters and a brother, they die of pneumonia.

But we come back.

Us Métis we are hard to kill.

Red River.

"I do that song this time," said Du Pré.

"Good," said Madelaine, "But I cry you know."

"That one part I don't figure out, it just come to me."

"Good," said Madelaine.

Du Pré had a little more whiskey.

He slowed down and he pulled off on a snowplow turn-around. He got his fiddle out of the case and he tuned it and he sat on the hood and he ran his fingers over the strings and he tightened the horsehair on his bow a little.

Du Pré played the song for Billy Grouard.

The melody looped and whirled and blended like a stream of clear water, and it was sad, like time is sad.

When he finished Madelaine was sobbing softly. She stopped and she wiped her eyes.

"What you call that song, Du Pré?" said Madelaine.

" 'Billy Drank the Gold,' " said Du Pré.

"Those fuckers," said Madelaine.

❧ CHAPTER 36 ❧

The high school gymnasium was jammed with people. Du Pré and Tally and Bassman were on, and the crowd was whooping and stomping and the security people were yelling desperately at those whooping and stomping in the bleachers to quit before the bleachers collapsed.

The three had been playing nonstop for thirty minutes. They ran out the last few bars of "Boiling Cabbage" and they quit and the cheering and the whistling started.

"That was some good fiddle," said Tally. He looked very happy. Bassman never changed expression.

"You guys very tight," said Du Pré, "Now we get the fuck out of this place stinks like old socks, find us a nice bar to play in maybe."

"Well," said Bassman, "We don't tell no one or we can't get in, they like this music plenty good."

Tally hefted his accordion case to his shoulder and he put his crutches on. He had new ones that had clips that went over his huge biceps. He was standing straighter and he had no pain in his face.

Du Pré lifted his small light fiddle case.

"I am smarter than you guys," he said. He looked at Bassman putting the covers over his amplifiers.

"Yah," said Bassman, "You so smart you get a bar fight what you going to do, that damn fiddle. I swing this bass they run, man." He grinned.

Du Pré helped him roll the amplifier away, then he took it while Bassman got his bass case and the little bag with the cords.

"Always get some fool to do it for me," said Bassman, catching up to Du Pré, who was hunkered over his load, "Some asshole only got a little fiddle case to carry."

They went out the side door and over to Bassman's van and they loaded up.

"Madelaine she is off with our car," said Du Pré, "So I maybe ride with you?"

"Sure," said Bassman, "We find that bar. A poor little bar for the poor Métis, one that maybe has a little back room, the gambling."

They got in and Bassman drove off to a roadhouse a mile or so out of town. There were a few cars there. Madelaine had brought the Rover and Bart's lovely old cruiser was sitting in plain view. Nice new tires.

"How you know this place?" said Du Pré.

Bassman grinned.

"Madelaine she tell me to come here after," said Bassman, "She say there is lots of pretty women here and it has this pretty big dance floor and a room upstairs where there is gambling. Not these chickenshit TVs got the cards, keno on them, got tables, maybe some craps on a blanket on the floor."

"Yah," said Du Pré.

"But there is a Stick Game up there tonight," said Bassman, "Pret' big money on it, you know them Gros Ventré women they are pret' good they play some Kiowa, some Sioux, some Osage."

Du Pré nodded.

"We better set up now," said Bassman, "We are not the only ones told about this. Another hour I bet you can't get in the door."

"Maybe they got chicken wire in front of the stage," grinned Tally, "Keep them Métis from bouncing beer bottles off us they don't like our music. Keep them Sioux from scalping us."

Du Pré helped Bassman carry his big amp in. They stood for a moment in the dimness and then saw a tiny stage off in an alcove. It was set well up off the floor. There were twin bearskins nailed to the wall on each side of it and a mounted sailfish high over the little stage. The sailfish had a lot of dollar bills stuck to it.

"Hey," said Du Pré, "This is a good place." A couple of women behind the bar grinned at Du Pré and Bassman. Madelaine and Bart and Gretchen were sitting at a little table under a tiny window.

"Do you own that lovely Land Rover?" yelled Bart.

Du Pré made a Métis sign for up-your-ass.

Du Pré went back and he got his fiddle case and he held the door for Tally as he sidled through with the heavy accordion. Bassman came behind him with the rest of his gear.

"Got some guitar players coming," said Tally, "Harmonica, even got a drummer. Not one of them drummer make a lot of noise, he is a skin drum guy, white guy but he is good. Play that pancake drum, medicine drum."

Du Pré nodded. If Bassman liked them he would too.

Du Pré walked over to where Bart and Madelaine and Gretchen were sitting. Bart was dressed in faded old ranch clothes and he had a chew of snoose in one cheek. He was sipping a soda. The women had some wine in stemmed glasses.

Du Pré looked at Bart.

"Damn," said Bart, "That cruiser is nice, just whips down the road. How was your trip?"

"Give me the fucking keys," said Du Pré, "I take back every mean thing I ever say, you. I am whipped. You beat me. I am not driving that Rover back home."

"But I like it," said Bart, "You bastard, you've been hiding the true pleasure of driving Montana roads from me, the idle rich."

"OK," said Du Pré, "Outside I whip your ass till I get those keys, I whip it plenty."

"But, Du Pré," said Gretchen, "You just aren't going to get that car away from Bart. He loves that car."

"Shit," said Du Pré, "Damn."

Madelaine was laughing.

Du Pré looked at Bart again.

"You want me to beg you, I do," said Du Pré, "I can't take no more of that damn Land Rover."

"This isn't even any fun anymore," said Bart, fishing a set of keys out of his jeans, "OK, you can't have mine. Yours is around back. It has a red ribbon on the radio antenna."

"Ah," said Du Pré, "My great friend Bart."

"He is a good friend," said Madelaine, "You two you quit now. Gretchen and me, we want to have a good time, not put up with you being kids."

Du Pré went out the side door and around behind the building. There was a police cruiser there, an old one with bald patches where the cop signs had been and sockets where the light bar fitted on to the roof. Du Pré got in and he put the key in the ignition and the engine caught right away and it roared and purred. There was a new radio. A holder. The holder was a round one but larger and deeper than a coffee cup holder. There were two elastic bands across the top opening.

Fifth of whiskey fit in it. Pint, too, the bands would hold it.

Du Pré laughed.

He got out and he opened the trunk.

There was a cooler, a box with several flashlights in it, and a big jeep bag. Two of them zipped together.

A fiddle case. An old one.

Du Pré opened it. He lifted the violin out. There was a note in the bottom.

"The car is in good shape, and this is supposed to be a good violin for the music you play so well. Thanks for being my friend. Bart."

Du Pré laughed. He tuned the fiddle and he played it a little.

A marvelous instrument. It seemed alive.

I use this on some of them ballads, Du Pré thought, it has that sad tone, better than mine.

243

He put the fiddle back in the case and he carried it back in.

"I thank you, Bart," he said, holding up the case.

"Sure," said Bart, "You give so much with that, I wondered if maybe you ever needed one to play while the one you have was being fixed."

Du Pré thought of the wedge of stove wood he had glued under a split place in the back, which didn't help the tone in the old one.

"Yah," he said, "I get the other one fixed now."

"Fixed?" said Madelaine, "It always sound good, me."

"Well," said Du Pré, "I have to stick some stuff in it. It is ready, fall apart I think."

Some of the binding on his old fiddle was loose, too, and even when he glued it it would not stay.

"Gretchen and me we drive the Rover back," said Madelaine, "Maybe take Jeanne home. Then I come back. I don't leave very quick, though, so you are not able to hustle new pussy tonight."

"Yah," said Du Pré.

"We better eat," said Bart, "I ordered some steaks and a bunch of shrimp. Pretty soon they will have to shut the kitchen down."

A waitress began bringing plates with big porterhouse steaks and piles of huge shrimp on them, and bowls of cole slaw and a pitcher of iced tea. There was plenty.

Du Pré and Bart and the women and Bassman and Tally ate and ate while people filed slowly into the bar.

Du Pré sat back, stuffed. He sipped some whiskey. He

rolled a smoke. He looked up at the ceiling, the boards had a few bullet holes in them.

Du Pré grinned.

He felt a tug on his sleeve, and he turned and looked.

There was a frail, beautiful child there, a girl, with huge dark eyes and the redflashed hair, black with fire in it, of the Assiniboines.

"My grandpapa asked me to ask you if you play, we dance?" she said, very shy.

"Sure we do that," said Du Pré. He got the new fiddle out.

Du Pré looked at the old white-haired man standing on the little dance floor with the little girl's hand in his.

Du Pré started the slow dance.

The old man stepped, smiling down at the little girl.

The little girl stared at the old man's feet and she followed his every move.

Red River.

❧ CHAPTER 37 ❧

Du Pré had taken his soaking shirt off and he had only his kerchief around his neck. He took a bar towel from a small pile on Bassman's amp and he mopped his face and hair and neck.

It was so hot and close in the bar, even with the windows and doors all open and a huge fan sucking in the kitchen that often Du Pré's eyes burned so badly halfway through a song from the sweat rolling into them he had trouble staying on measure.

Finally Madelaine walked up and she tied her silk scarf around his head to make him a sweatband. She kissed Du Pré and then threaded her way through the people back to the little table where she and Bart and Gretchen were sitting. Bart had placed two chairs up on the table so that Gretchen and Madelaine could sit and see over the heads of the people who were jammed together throughout the rest of the bar.

Some people had gone out to the parking lot to dance and fight.

Du Pré's fingers ached.

A singer and guitar player from Turtle Mountain was waiting to go on. Another fiddler, too. Du Pré was damned glad of it. They could have the last hour and a half before the bar had to close and empty itself of people.

Du Pré finished the song and he looked at Tally and Bassman and he shrugged.

"I quit," he said, "My fingers they are bleeding." They were, the skin worn through on a couple.

They had been playing for eight hours steadily. The Turtle Mountain people hadn't shown up until very late. An old car, it had broken down and they had had trouble getting rides.

"Yeah," said Bassman, "Me, I can play this thing for days."

Tally grinned.

Du Pré cased his old fiddle up in the rawhide case with the quill-work on it and he grabbed his shirt and a couple towels and he went through the crowd to Madelaine and Bart and Gretchen.

"Pret' good music there, Du Pré," said Madelaine. She leaned over and kissed him a long time.

"My fella," she said, pointing a finger into his chest and tapping.

Du Pré laughed.

"I am going outside," said Du Pré, "I got to cool off." They were pretty near the open side door. People were coming in and going out.

"I come," said Madelaine, "I got this drink for you." She had a beer stein filled with ice and whiskey and water.

They went outside. People were standing in the lot,

leaned on cars. Far back toward the uncut hayfield a pair of men were fighting, but they were both drunk and they kept missing when they swung. They were alone.

There was a sudden yell from the room upstairs where the Stick Game was going on.

Du Pré looked up at the open window. He could see a couple people standing there, and then a little bit of a mangy-looking painted ceiling.

Another yell.

Then there was a long song, an ululation and a chanting.

Madelaine grinned at Du Pré.

"I can't get up there," said Madelaine, "But Jeanne and her people they are winning. They win and win and win. Someone say that there is five thousand dollars on the blanket once. They are doing mighty good. That Jeanne she is singing good tonight, telling that good story."

Du Pré nodded.

The crowd upstairs began to whistle and cheer.

"Me, I am not going back in there," said Du Pré. Even though it was cool outside he was still running sweat. He had a big gulp of his drink. The whiskey bloomed warm in his belly.

"They are happy plenty," said Madelaine, "Hey, where are we staying this night."

"We got a motel room," said Du Pré, "But me, I would rather we drive off someplace and sleep out. There is a big jeep bag in the trunk of the cruiser."

"Prolly we can't sleep much that motel," said Madelaine, "These people they will have a good time all night."

Bart and Gretchen came out into the night air.

248

"We're gonna go," said Bart, "It's just too hot in here. That guitar guy sings good. But, Christ it is hot there."

Gretchen looked as pressed and cool as if she was in an air-conditioned limousine.

Du Pré wondered how she managed that.

"Yah," said Du Pré, "I think that we go out, find a piece of grass to sleep on tonight. The motel will be noisy."

"There's some bags in the trunk," said Bart. He grinned.

Du Pré put his fiddle case in the cruiser and he got in and he drove slowly out into the hayfield. The field had a road through it, just a pair of tracks, and Du Pré got on to them and they wound around behind a pair of sheds and then they came out on to the road.

They drove up into the Snowy Mountains. There were Forest Service campgrounds off the dirt road. Near the top they found one that was nothing but some stone firepits and a couple outhouses and the road rutted enough so that the big motor homes couldn't get in. They drove to a campsite screened by a low hedge of pines. The trees were bent at the base, all twisted, so the snows were deep here, in the winter.

Du Pré and Madelaine sat on the hood of the car looking up at the black sky shot with bright stars.

A green comet shot across the sky and it burned out.

It was very quiet.

Du Pré fished a fresh shirt out of his bag and he put it on. The night air was cutting and there might even be a little frost on the grass in the morning.

Madelaine sucked on a bottle of pink wine and Du Pré sipped whiskey and he smoked.

A bear snuffed by, out of sight in the trees, looking for something to eat. The sounds of its feet died away.

"Pret' nice up here," said Madelaine. "I heard that Billy Grouard he will be out of the hospital soon, they take him to jail then."

"Yah," said Du Pré, "Dumb kid, he sure mess his life up there. Shoot those two guys, who are just there earning wages."

"Well," said Madelaine. "Bart he is helping find Billy a lawyer."

"He will do that, Bart," said Du Pré.

"Bart is kind," said Madelaine.

"He is too kind," said Du Pré, "How long you think that he owns this cruiser he give me?"

"Oh," said Madelaine, "He buy three a long time ago, have them engine all fixed, everything. He like doing that."

"Yeah," said Du Pré, "You see that Jeanne at all?"

"We talk a little, before she go up to the Stick Game," said Madelaine. "I think she be OK now, she sure want to win. She say she have a new story."

Du Pré nodded.

"Story about Danny and Billy and the poison water," said Madelaine, "I have not heard it."

"Ah," said Du Pré, "She maybe be all right then."

"You play me that song about Billy some time. I know that your fingers they are very sore now."

"Yeah, me, I have too good a time tonight," said Du Pré.

"You like them crowds," said Madelaine, "All them

pretty women they want to sleep with you you play so good. Tough for them, I am sorry."

Du Pré laughed.

A light plane flew past ten miles away, the lights on the wings and tail blinking.

Du Pré went to the rear of the cruiser and he got the jeep bags out and he took a flashlight and he found a patch of thick grass and he tossed a couple sticks and some rocks out and he unrolled the bags. They were new, and covered in waxed canvas with flannel linings.

A little wind picked up and the pines soughed and the smell of the sap perfumed the breeze. An owl called softly.

"Him hunting," said Du Pré to Madelaine, "He call and a bird get scared and move on the branch and the owl know."

They undressed and crawled into the bag. It was soft and warm and the grass was a good mattress.

"Some nice motel we got here," said Madelaine, "Plenty of that fresh air, not too stale and run through no damn air conditioner."

"Nice here," said Du Pré.

"Too high for them," said Madelaine.

"So Jeanne she is singing about Danny and Billy," said Du Pré, "Tell that story, I guess. That will win her some she tell it good."

"She is doing that," said Madelaine, "I talk to this woman who is watching them and she say Jeanne she cannot be beat, she run them Kiowa around so bad they lose all their money this afternoon, probably leave. Also the gambling is not so legal I guess, there are state cops want to stop it all, state is not getting its cut I guess."

"Yah," said Du Pré, "They like them damn TV card games, keno."

"That Bart he will be happy with Gretchen," said Madelaine.

"How you know that?" said Du Pré.

"She tell me he is gonna be," said Madelaine.

"Yah," said Du Pré, "Well that is good for Bart."

"He is a nice man," said Madelaine.

"So am I," said Du Pré.

"I am tired, talking," said Madelaine.

"Sure," said Du Pré.

They looked up at the stars for a while.

"Me," said Madelaine, "I sneak upstairs see that game."

Du Pré grunted.

"Don't want you to think I don't like that music you play."

"Christ," said Du Pré, "You listen to it so much you maybe get bored. Once a while, I get bored."

"Jeanne she does best," said Madelaine.

Du Pré rolled a smoke and he waited.

✤ CHAPTER 38 ✤

It is maybe the way them Assiniboines play," said Madelaine. "They got the twenty-one sticks, the stone. Jeanne she lets Mallee start. Mallee she jump around, she wriggle, them Cheyenne, their leader makes her guess, it is the right hand. So they lose a stick. They lose some more, Jeanne she is sitting all still. They lose twelve stick, Mallee she cannot guess right once. Cheyennes are singing a powerful song, lots of money on the blanket, notes betting horses, cars . . ."

Them Indians gamblers, for sure, Du Pré thought, whole villages bet everything, century ago, lost all of it.

Us Métis we gamble some, too.

"Mallee she is singing louder, then Jeanne take her place. She starts to sing about Danny and the poison water. She guess right, takes all them sticks back. They are even, Jeanne picks up five more. Then them Cheyenne put their best singer in. Jeanne, her, they sing, Jeanne picks the right hand."

Du Pré thought of all the Stick Games he had seen. No two were ever that much alike.

"Cheyenne she is pret' good singer, Jeanne is better. Cheyenne sing a song, Jeanne goes on, the poison water, the gold. Cheyennes they are much worried. Don't do them no good. Jeanne takes sixteen more sticks and that game is over. Lot of money change hands, there. Lot of money."

Jeanne rout them, Du Pré thought, not that much story there.

"Jeanne she reaches over, hands back the bundle, they start again. Plenty money on the blanket, ever'body watching close. Jeanne she guess right. She hand back some sticks before the game is over. Keeps on singing her long song, then she start to tell the story of Billy Grouard. She take from them Cheyennes she give some back, she does that till she is done, and then she gets up, says the game is over. Everybody is looking, they don't know what she means. She walks away, Mallee sits, another woman takes Jeanne's place, then them Gros Ventré lose that game."

Stick Games could move fast or slow.

Gambling, poetry, theater, songs, noisy and colorful.

Whites sit around a table, see who can have no expression at all, Du Pré thought. They are a people who hate fun.

I am glad I am Métis. Don't got to go through life, a cob up my ass.

"Some them Big Bellies say that Jeanne, she is maybe the best Stick Game player ever. You know they talk 'bout what she done? Once she just sit, keep the stone the same hand, lose fourteen stick, then she wins back the stone, she starts to sing, old Buffalo Hunting Song, she grab them Kiowa's medicine out of the air, she has everything on her blanket, five minutes."

Du Pré looked up at the stars in the blue-black night sky.

"She is some genius," said Madelaine.

A bullbat clacked overhead, the hard pinion feathers slapping together.

Du Pré loved the funny-looking birds, short wide beaks, eat only at night, gravel up at sunset, you could find them on the roadside filling their crops. Then they would find a light and fly back and forth through the cloud of moths and bugs, eating.

"Du Pré," said Madelaine, "You are listening to me?"

"Yah," said Du Pré.

"Genius is a white word. You know what it means."

Du Pré remembered his Latin, the nun who taught him.

"Possessed by a tutelary god," said Du Pré.

He had flunked a test once by saying it meant really smart.

"What is tutelary?" said Madelaine.

"Teacher," said Du Pré.

"How you get so smart?"

"Flunk one of Sister Michael's tests, you get a lot smarter in a big hurry," said Du Pré.

"She hit you?"

"No," said Du Pré.

"What she do?"

"She say, *Gabriel you are disappointing me.*"

Madelaine laughed and laughed.

"More than forty years, you still love that nun," said Madelaine.

"Yah," said Du Pré, laughing, "She is a ver' good teacher. She say to me Du Pré you are a Métis and you got a proud history you ought to know more about. She bring me books.

I am playing music, she teach me how to read music a little. She is a kind person."

Some of the nuns and brothers at the school hadn't liked the Indians or the Métis. The children knew. But Sister Michael loved them. The children knew that, too.

"Fiddlers pret' crazy like Jeanne," said Madelaine, "the good ones anyway."

Du Pré laughed and laughed.

Red Sash Ramboulliette, friend of Catfoot's, old man when Du Pré met him, his life is playing the fiddle better than anyone, when he is out of the insane asylum.

Ever' once in a while Red Sash walk up the street waving his dick, shouting he plays with this!

Go and get a blanket, the people say, time for the priest take Red Sash off, a little rest.

"You are thinking of Red Sash," said Madelaine.

"Yah," said Du Pré.

"I never know him but I hear him all the time, your music," said Madelaine.

Du Pré nodded.

Lots of people I don't even know in my music, dead thousands of years.

Long time gone the Breton French, the Welsh, the Scottish Islanders come here, before that Columbus.

De Champlain he is discovering the Saint Lawrence River, he passes a thousand Basque fishing boats in the Gulf.

Fiddle in Brittany, fiddle on the ocean, decks of little boats, fiddle in America, the shores of rivers, the prairie.

Them women dance, the buffalo hides pegged to the ground. Play the hand drum, like the Irish use.

Long time gone.

"Them stars look down a long time," said Madelaine, "See a lot."

The temperature was dropping. Madelaine moved very close to Du Pré, put her head on his chest, the bedroll was warm.

"Maybe we can't help that Jeanne," said Madelaine.

"Maybe she just need, go away once in a while, like Red Sash," said Du Pré.

"People want to make her well," said Madelaine.

"Maybe she is well," said Du Pré, "need to go and rest, get herself put together, once a while."

"Du Pré," said Madelaine, "You tell me a story now."

Du Pré laughed.

Madelaine loved to put her head on his chest, hear his voice rumble.

"Long time gone," said Du Pré . . .

Everything was made by the Grandfathers and Grandmothers but all the living things were down beneath the earth.

Outside the sun shone and the moon held the night and the grass and stones and trees were made, and the seas and waters flowed, but there were none of the Peoples, the Six-Leggeds, Four-Leggeds, Bird Peoples, Two-Leggeds.

It is time for them to come on up, so they start out and the Great Bear is leading them, the Buffalo behind the Great Bear.

257

All the Peoples are pret' happy, it is dark and cold down there.

They walk a long time and they are getting near the opening of the cave leads out on to the Earth.

But they find a huge round boulder blocking the path.

The Great Bear he roars and bites and shoves but the stone is too big even for him.

The human beings try but they are too weak.

Then the Buffalo say, let us try. Buffalo are maybe the size of big dogs then.

The other peoples wait.

Coyote he listens to the Buffalo and he leads everybody, a big dance, they call on the Grandmothers, Grandfathers, help the Buffalo.

Buffalo they are that size, so that a Buffalo is a good supper, a big family.

The Grandmothers, Grandfathers listen, they talk, they agree they made a mistake.

Mistakes they happen all the time.

The little Buffalo all put their heads, the stone.

The Peoples pray.

The Buffalo bellow and paw the earth and shove and then they begin to grow. Big Buffalo weighs a hundred pounds maybe.

They shove and then they begin to grow.

Bulls they weigh a ton and a half, time the growing is done.

They are given big shoulders, push that stone.

They bellow and paw the earth and they roll that stone

up and out on to the earth easy as a dog noses a horse turd along the ground.

Every People comes out into the light and then the world.

"That is how the buffalo got, so big," said Du Pré.

"Catfoot," said Madelaine. "He tell that story, his little boy can go to sleep.

"Me, I don't want to sleep yet," she said.

"Yah," said Du Pré.

❖ CHAPTER 39 ❖

The Stick Game was still going on when Du Pré and Madelaine drove back into Lewistown. They stopped at a trucker's restaurant and had breakfast and Du Pré gassed up the old cruiser. Then they drove past the roadhouse and saw the upstairs window open and a guy with a big ass was sitting on the ledge. They got out and walked over and they could hear Jeanne's strong voice singing.

There were some people in the parking lot sitting on or in their cars, looking tired and most of them hungover. The bar was open and the doors and windows were wide.

Du Pré passed by one of the windows and a gust of stale beery air flew past. The bar would take a long time to air out and before it did Du Pré thought that he would be back in it playing to a packed crowd.

But it was a lot of fun. There had been some very good dancing the night before and the drummer was wonderful, playing the old skin drums with a wrapped stick and adding old rhythms that Du Pré knew came from a time long before the whites even knew where the Americas were.

Long time ago. Very long time.

"You want to go over to the festival, Du Pré?" said Madelaine.

"No," said Du Pré, "The way it is run, all those things, classrooms, sit with your mouth just right. Very boring. I went, grade school. No, I like it here. Play some music, maybe I even play some cards, what you want to do, though?"

"Same thing," said Madelaine, laughing, "Who are those funny guys keep wandering around asking all those questions, got the clipboards?"

"They are either anthropologists or them folklorists," said Du Pré, "Bart show me a book they publish. Got some of my songs in it, say they were written in the seventeenth century, eighteenth century, nineteenth century—author unknown. News to me, I do not know I am four centuries old. Me, I remember I write those songs last twenty years or so. I think I did, anyway."

"Hee," said Madelaine, "OK, they ask me those questions I give them some answers, you bet."

Du Pré nodded. Some poor bastard was in for it.

"That is all right?"

"Yah, Du Pré," said Madelaine, "It is fine. There are some real fine people here. I wonder where that Bart and Gretchen are?"

Du Pré looked around. The other cruiser was gone but the expensive Rover was still sitting there.

"They be back," said Du Pré.

"I will go up and watch that Stick Game," said Madelaine, "You come?"

Du Pré nodded. They went inside and up the stairs. The room was still full, and people were hunched over and looking very intently at the eight women on blankets who were facing each other, four on a side.

The Gros Ventré team was up, and Jeanne was singing her song, the woman directly across from her held the sticks in two bundles, one in each hand.

Jeanne finished and a woman from the other team replied, carrying the story forward.

The woman sang Jimmy and Mickey halfway through the night on the plains with a thunderstorm coming and she stopped and raised her hands palm up.

Jeanne nodded and she sang the song to its end, with Jimmy and Mickey back in camp and not lost any more and the women taking care of them, they were hungry and scratched and beaten by their ordeal, but they had won.

"Seven, fourteen," said Jeanne, fingers pointing at the woman who was holding the sticks.

She held her hands up, with the bundles of sticks, and she laid them down on the blanket and she counted the ones in her right hand.

Seven.

Fourteen in the left.

Jeanne ululated. The teammate who was nearest the money piled on the blanket at the end scooped it up and she dumped the bills into a beaded bag.

The team that had lost rose and they began to gather their things and stretch. They had been sitting crosslegged for hours.

"How she do that?" said Du Pré.

"Strong medicine," said Madelaine, "You see her move

her hand that last time, grab all them other medicine right out of the air. Whoomph. Like that. She plays very good, get them women give up their game."

"How much there is in that bag?" said Du Pré.

"A bunch," said Madelaine.

Du Pré grinned at her.

A young woman with red hair dressed in worn denims and boots whipped a paper out of her jacket pocket and a badge out of her purse and she announced that the place was busted and that she was arresting all of those which she had seen gambling and all eight members of the Stick Game teams.

There were three male cops in plain clothes with her and sirens wound in as more police arrived. There were state police and local police and sheriff's deputies.

Jeanne's face burned red. She was enraged.

Du Pré and Madelaine watched and Jeanne calmed down. She held out her wrists for the handcuffs and she walked downstairs behind a couple of the women from the other team. The police had a school bus parked near the bar and all of those arrested filed up the steps and they sat waiting for the police to bring their friends who also wore handcuffs, the light plastic kind.

The redhaired young woman cop dumped the blankets and gambling sticks into big black plastic garbage bags and tagged them. The money was put in a locking briefcase.

"This is not lawful in Montana," said the redhaired young woman, "Don't try this again here. Now this bar is going to be closed pending a hearing and they may be closed permanently. They may lose their license. This is a serious matter."

"Oh, yeah," said Du Pré.

"You'll all have to leave now," said the woman cop.

Du Pré and Madelaine filed downstairs with the others and they went outside. People were milling around and cursing.

The big yellow schoolbus ground away with its load of arrested Indian and Métis.

"Some festival huh?" said Madelaine, "This some festival. They are hurting no one, and this?"

Du Pré nodded.

"Chickenshit," said Madelaine.

Du Pré looked down the street. Bart's cruiser was headed their way. Bart pulled up into the lot and he rolled down his window.

"What the fuck is this?" he said.

"They arrest all the Stick Game people," said Du Pré, "They maybe don't do that on the res, you know, but they sure do here."

"Christ," said Bart.

"Bart," said Du Pré, "These people mostly don't got no money. If they have to post bail they will not have it, have to sit in jail till there is a trial."

"Sure," said Bart, "I'll bail 'em, no problem."

"Who are they hurting, Bart?" said Madelaine, "Fucking cops, they want this Métis festival here? Us Métis gamble, you know, I was about to maybe put some money, the Stick Game later. I do that you had been bailing me out of jail."

"Well," said Bart, "I doubt the police were happy about it."

"They seem pretty happy," said Madelaine.

"Someone complained," said Bart. He looked across the road to a low cinderblock building.

JESUS SAVES, a sign said in letters four feet high on the roof. There was a fat man in a cheap suit standing in front of the building, looking happy.

"And there he is," said Bart, "Another Christer. God damn, it makes them so happy when they can spoil other folks's fun."

Du Pré grunted.

"Shit," he said, "I don't want to stay here no more. This was a good festival, people liking the music, good Stick Game, now this. Me, I don't want to play no damn gymnasium."

A couple of plainclothes cops were putting court seals over the doors of the roadhouse. The two women who had tended the bar were standing outside and weeping.

"They are doing a good thing," said Madelaine, "Look at this."

"If it is against the law they got to do this, the police," said Du Pré, "It is no good but they don't got a choice."

The fat Christer across the street had been joined by a couple of his congregants. They all were smiling, happy, they'd done the Lord's Work.

"We'd have just not noticed this," said one of the cops, "But the Reverend over there raised some hell and signed a complaint. This is all such bullshit. It was a good thing, this festival, and now I guess it won't happen again."

265

"What about the bail?" said Bart.

"Oh," said the cop, "Judge Morris won't set any I don't think. I expect it'll all die away. But it'll kill the festival, too."

"Us Métis," said Madelaine, "We don't got a reservation."

The cops got in a tan car and they drove off.

"Let's go home, Du Pré," said Madelaine.

"You got to drive the Rover," said Du Pré.

"I wait for Jeanne," said Madelaine, "Take her home."

"Shit," said Bart.

✤ CHAPTER 40 ✤

It's all there," said Piney, "all three labs. Horrible levels of lead, cadmium, selenium—Persephone pumps and Persephone spills and anything downstream starts having babies with three heads and no legs. Look at these. Look at these!"

Pat Weller was flicking his eyes over the computer printouts. His face was sad and his lips were tight.

"Unspeakable," he said, "The injection well. Christ, without knowing the volumes pumped . . . but I'd expect this crud is going to be showing up in the groundwater far and wide for decades."

"I wonder any of them see Mickey or Danny Bouyer," said Du Pré, "Or they think of Billy Grouard, who does murder because of them."

"No," said Pat Weller, "What they see is bad public relations which may lead to losses."

"That selenium is bad shit," said Piney, "Lots of folks will end up with dishrag heart. Selenium messes up the electrical circuits. The heart gets flabby trying to pump. I suppose that'll never come out, since it won't show up for twenty, thirty years."

"So where do we go?" said Piney, "Sue the bastards?"

"Yes," said Pat Weller, "And that will take years and in the meantime Persephone will go right on doing this. Worse comes to worse when the court judgments don't go their way they can just declare bankruptcy and walk off. The People of the United States will get to pay for cleaning it all up."

Du Pré laughed. "Me, I never thought I would be no environmentalist," he said, "And I am one I guess."

"Oh," said Piney, "That wolf crap. Sure turned out bad down in Yellowstone."

"Yah," said Du Pré.

"On to the lawyers," said Pat Weller.

"The second guy that Billy shoot he just die," said Du Pré, "So it is two counts of murder he has."

"Well," said Piney, "I'm going down to the bar and kick the shit out of Norris, damn it, I need my friend."

"I go with you," said Du Pré.

"I'll join you," said Pat Weller, "I believe I was to meet Alla there, and Gretchen and Bart. They've been up at the dig."

"Bart he get that other place yet?" said Du Pré.

"Haven't heard," said Pat Weller, "But I expect that he will."

They drove down to the little saloon separately. The rain was coming down very hard, fall rain, and it smelled of snow. The mountains would have caps of white and the birds would flock now and leave soon.

Du Pré was the last to come in. He shook the rain from his hat and he put it back on.

Piney and Norris were talking earnestly, and Norris was pounding his fist into his palm.

"Well," said Bart, looking up at Du Pré, "I guess we start making the lawyers rich now."

"Sue them a bunch," said Du Pré, "Me, I never think like that before."

"It'll take seven years at least," said Pat Weller, "And they'll fight every fact, every reading, every sample. That company is worth billions and they won't miss a trick."

"Soon's this rain lets up," hollered Piney, "I want to fly over the mine. Something going on there."

Du Pré nodded.

They all talked of nothing much and even watched some stupid game show on the television.

The sun broke through and a wind came up and dried the grass in a few minutes.

Piney and Norris and Pat Weller and Du Pré went out to the veterinary hospital and they piled into Piney's light plane.

"Let's lighten the plane," said Piney, as he taxied around and got ready to take off, "when we pass the windsock there throw Norris out. I should be doing seventy by then."

"Har de har har," said Norris, "my good friend."

They raced down the dirt runway and Piney pulled the plane into the air and they cleared the barbwire fence by a good two feet.

"I've missed that fence hundreds of times," said Piney, "But one of these days I won't."

"I'll sew you back together," said Norris, "I promise."

Piney flew west over the low mountains, and he headed over the dig site. They could see Big Jim Lascaux waving far below and the bare patches where the tents had stood. The camp was pretty well broken down and would wait a few months before the snows went and it was time to start again.

A little farther on two dirt bike riders were cutting tracks in the thin soil of the Sweetgrass Hills.

"You got one of them shotguns on this thing," said Norris, "The kind for shooting coyotes from the plane."

"No," said Piney, "But I'll get a couple. Look at those pricks. That grass won't come back for a century."

Piney turned toward the mine.

Far to the west the Chinook Arch crossed the sky.

Du Pré looked at the light. The land below was glowing with it and he could see the winds track the grass far below.

"Some fine country," said Piney, "Tough country but good country."

"Good to ride on," said Norris.

The mine was just up ahead.

Piney flew low and they passed over the settling pond, unearthly turquoise, lower than usual. The sides of the banks were still damp from a drawdown.

"Look at that," said Pat Weller.

Workmen were tearing the siding off the buildings that housed the giant pumps for the injection well.

"I thought so," said Pat Weller, "They are going to obliterate any trace of that well. Jesus. We got a camera on this plane?"

Piney handed him a 35mm with a telephoto lens.

270

"We have to fly over every day a couple times," said Weller, "We have to have a record of this."

"How will they deny that it was ever there?" said Norris, "Just flat lie, I suppose."

"Jesus," said Pat Weller, "I never expected this. They must have pumped the lake down and now they are going to wait on the courts. They'll just let the discharges go now, right on top."

"They do this?" said Du Pré, "They cannot be stopped?"

"No," said Pat Weller, "They can't."

"Christ," said Du Pré, "What this do to the suing? What it do in court?"

"Argue about whether the injection well was there at all," said Pat Weller, "That's what they'll do. And the guys tearing that down do have real job security. Boy, do they."

"Why don't the State do something?" said Du Pré, "Since they are poisoning people."

"You tuck arsenic in Madelaine's pink wine," said Pat Weller, "And you will do time. They poison whole counties and say . . . what, us?"

"Get some shots," said Piney, dropping the plane.

Pat Weller ran a roll of film. He replaced the film and he handed the shot film to Norris, who penned a date and time on the tab.

They flew back and forth for a half hour, snapping pictures.

"Until tomorrow," said Piney. He turned back toward Malta.

The black clouds to the west were closing fast.

Piney set the little plane down on the dirt runway two minutes before the wind at the front of the new storm broke.

Du Pré and Norris and Pat Weller held on to the plane while Piney guyed the wings and tail down. He tied the last knot and the four of them ran for the veterinary hospital. Hail rattled down hard, some of the ice blobs the size of baseballs.

"Nice new dents in my plane," said Piney.

"The insurance'll pay for it," said Weller.

"What insurance?" said Piney.

They both laughed.

Du Pré drove back down to the bar and he went in. Bart and Gretchen had left.

"They were headed for Toussaint," said the woman behind the bar, "And they said to tell you that they would see you there."

Du Pré nodded.

"I take a whiskey ditch," he said.

Du Pré sat at the bar a while, listening to the storm outside and the wind that would gust cold wet air into the warm room.

He was the only person in the bar.

Finally he went out and he got in the cruiser and he headed home. The storm was lifting and he got the car up to eighty in a hurry and each time he would come to the bottom of a stretch of road there would be water over it and he would have to brake and even at forty he sent up long roostertails of water when the tires crashed into the floods over the roadway. Some of them were a foot and a half deep.

Du Pré sipped a little whiskey and he rolled himself a cigarette and he drove in the fresh clean air that smelled of lightning.

He whistled for a while, the song that he had written for Billy Grouard.

The water on the road drained away and he made better time.

He got to Toussaint just at dark.

The bar had a lot of people in it.

Du Pré went in, and he walked up behind Madelaine and he hugged her.

✤ CHAPTER 41 ✤

The van shot through the night. Du Pré drove, not liking the automatic transmission. It was too smooth. The one on the old cruiser at least shuddered a little when the bands shifted so that you knew it was there.

There were three more behind him.

"This be some fun, Du Pré," said Madelaine. She was dressed up in her velvets and turquoise jewelry. She had a beaded headband on and wrist cuffs and a wide silver belt of sandcast crooked strips.

"We bust their ass," said Jeanne, laughing. He and her chums for the Stick Game were sitting in the back seats. One of them had a small drum and they would sing from time to time.

"That Bart he have some good ideas," said Du Pré.

"That Bart he own a bunch of TV stations," said Madelaine, "So at least we get paid some attention, yes."

Du Pré dodged to miss a jackrabbit scuttling across the blacktop. The night was young and black with some high cloud.

"There it is," said Madelaine, looking at the glow on the horizon. "Keep that place lit up all night, fools."

"Mine runs around the clock," said Du Pré, "Get that gold out."

Jeanne and her chums ululated for a long time.

It made Du Pré's head ache. He sipped some whiskey and he rolled himself a smoke.

He turned off on the road that led to the mine's main gates and he slowed until all three of the other vans turned off behind him.

"OK," he said, "We got to get there and swing them gates shut and chain them up and then we will start."

He crested the hill and the road wound down to a cyclone fence with a gate and a guard's booth on the road.

A security guard stepped out of the booth and he looked at Du Pré's little caravan and then he ran back to the booth to raise an alarm. The gates began to swing shut on their cables.

"Good!" said Du Pré, "They are doing it for us!"

Du Pré drove right up to the gates and he waited until they met and locked and then he jumped out with some chain and he wrapped the chain around the pipes and he padlocked the chains.

The guard didn't come out of his booth. Some flashing yellow lights started down toward the gate from the mine.

Bart got out of the second van. He dragged a bundle of clothesrods sharpened at one end to the gate and then he went back for a sledgehammer and he and Du Pré pounded the long stakes into the hard earth.

Jeanne and her women friends and Madelaine hung feathered tops on the stakes. The feathered stakes marched across the road.

"Looks holy," said Bart.

"Yah," said Du Pré, "It is how the Indians drive them

275

antelope, so I guess it is. These are turkey feathers, though. Not a big medicine bird, that turkey."

"Now, now," said Bart, "They taste a lot better than eagles for one thing."

The other two vans were full of TV camera crews and reporters. They were geared up and ready.

Jeanne and her women friends spread blankets on the ground in front of the feathered stakes and they began to sing and pass the little drum around.

"What are they saying?" said Bart.

"I don't got no Gros Ventré," said Du Pré, "You ask that Madelaine."

"They singing that all Persephone guys got little peckers and their wives fuck goats," said Madelaine.

"Yah," said Du Pré, "I thought so."

The TV crews moved forward, the cameramen and reporters coming right up to Jeanne and her friends. They waited respectfully for the song to end.

"What they singing now?" said Du Pré to Madelaine.

"All Persephone guys buttfuck their mothers with broomhandles," said Madelaine, "That is the clean part there, I am too embarrassed to talk about the rest, I am a nice Catholic girl."

Pat and Alla Weller were standing off to the side, smiling sadly.

Bart stood grinning hugely.

"I hope they fucking arrest me," he said, "I own so much Persephone stock now it would be my deepest heart's desire."

"I go now," said Madelaine. She walked over and stood in

front of Jeanne and her friends, who sang much more softly. They sang something that made Madelaine laugh and laugh.

"OK," she said, turning around and waving a finger at Jeanne, "I can not do this, you make me laughing all the time."

Jeanne and her chums hummed.

A reporter asked Madelaine what they were doing.

"We are protesting," said Madelaine, "We are mothers some of us got kids crippled by the poisons from this mine. Some got minds that don't work right from the poisons at this mine. We want this damn mine shut down and we want Persephone pay for helping these poor kids they poison."

The reporter spoke for a moment looking directly into the camera.

"What poison?" said the reporter to Madelaine.

"That Dr. Weller he tell you," said Madelaine, moving aside.

Pat Weller, in a suit and tie, hauled an easel over and he set it up and Alla handed him a placard with a list of the heavy metals leached from the ore into the groundwater on it.

Pat explained what they did.

Alla handed him large blown-up pictures of deformed animals.

Pat explained where and how this had happened.

Du Pré looked through the fence. The mine superintendant and his flunkies were conferring, heads together.

There were distant sirens headed toward the mine. The sheriff's department had been summoned.

Jeanne Bouyer got up and she came to Pat Weller and when Pat was done she looked at the camera and she looked at all the world and she began to speak in her deep clear voice.

"I am a woman got three kids," she said, "One is dead he kill himself little time ago. He is sick don't know why, he get sad and he kill himself. I got a beautiful daughter can't speak and can't hear. I got a boy who has trouble with his school-work. They are all born after I live near water that is bad. The mine say it is not them, but this all happen after they start."

The reporter turned to the camera again and she spoke for a moment.

Madelaine came back to the front and Jeanne sat with her friends and they began to sing again.

"What do the stakes mean?" said the reporter, looking at the feathered clothesrods.

"Medicine stakes," said Madelaine, "For all the kids killed, made simple by this mine. That mine, it send trucks over these stakes it is crushing these souls is what we believe."

Damn, thought Du Pré, That is very good bullshit, is what I believe. My Madelaine she is very good at this.

Ver' good. Me, I love this girl.

"They build a well, pump the bad water down deep in the earth," said Madelaine, "So that bad water it come up many miles from here, it come up for many years. They poison this whole land here, you know. Land is sacred, it is sick land now, they do this."

The reporter explained what an injection well was.

"Persephone denies that there was ever an injection well on their property," said the reporter, "But we have obtained

278

photographs of such a well, as it was being dismantled hastily."

"What will you do," said the reporter, "Stay here and block the road?"

"I got to go home take care of my poor sick kids," said Jeanne, "I would stay but I could not you see. Other people they stay, I got to go take care of my kids sick because of Persephone."

Kick them in the balls, Du Pré thought, you rip their damn dicks off there Jeanne. Yes.

"So we protest," said Madelaine, "Also Persephone wants to dig up, chew up the Sweetgrass Hills. That is sacred land, we believe, when we die, we go to the Sweetgrass Hills."

Good, Du Pré thought, my little Catholic girl here she is lying like a good woman. That hurt. I die, I don't got no idea where I go, but probably not there. Hee.

"My son Danny," said Jeanne, and the cameras all turned to her, "He kill himself, he throw himself in a well, we don't know what happen to him, then that Du Pré he find him."

The reporter looked at Du Pré, who fingered his fiddle.

"Poor Billy Grouard," said Jeanne, "He go crazy, drinking poison water, shoot a couple of mine guys. That Du Pré he write a song for Billy."

Du Pré started in and he fiddled the sad song he had written for Billy. The violin's sharp sweet notes rose and looped and Du Pré lost himself in the music. He played to the end.

For that Billy, Du Pré thought.

For everyone.

❖ CHAPTER 42 ❖

The charter buses had come and the Indians and the Métis were getting on but not very fast.

They were in Lodgepole.

"This is fun," said Jeanne, "Bart we thank you."

"Pleasure," said Bart.

Lawyer Charles Foote stood in the dust, looking at the sagebrush and open country with distaste.

Bart had given one million dollars worth of Persephone stock to the tribes.

The buses were on their way to the stockholders' meeting in San Francisco.

Which promised to be much more interesting than usual.

"Poor Billy," said Madelaine.

Billy Grouard had hung himself in his cell.

Best thing for him, Du Pré thought, good day to die.

"I am going to get outraged telephone calls from colleagues," said Lawyer Foote, obviously looking forward to those happy events.

Foote was wearing expensive clothing and shoes that shone like a waxed hardwood floor.

"Those Lobbs?" said Bart, innocently.

"Of course," said Foote.

"How much them Lobbs cost?" said Madelaine.

"Oh," said Foote, "a few dollars."

"Three thousand dollars," said Bart.

"This suit?" said Madelaine, "Who make it?"

"Huntsman," said Bart, "About four grand, maybe five."

"Foote," said Madelaine, "you are wearing eight thousand dollars?"

"With the watch," said Bart, "Closer to thirty."

"Christ," said Madelaine, "that is silly."

Foote looked at all of them. His eyes narrowed. Something was up and whatever it was Foote was going to absolutely *hate* it.

Bart's private jet flew low overhead and roared off to the east, the pilot wagging the wings a little.

Foote nodded.

"Du Pré," said Foote, "I am in need of your services. Price no object KILL THIS GUINEA PRICK!"

"Now Charles," said Bart, "Don't be a sore loser."

"Yah," said Jeanne, "We got a nice seat, the bus for you."

"I got your bag, my car," said Du Pré.

Foote walked to Du Pré's old cruiser and he opened the door and he took out his bag and he went in to the saloon and he was gone five minutes and when he came back out he was wearing old soft clothes and deck shoes.

No watch.

"There is going to be a payback," said Foote, "I will track you all down like coyotes."

"You'd have to do it here," said Bart, "And you dislike sagebrush, cactus, that sort of thing."

"Perhaps," said Foote.

"Did you find the Laphroaig I put in the bag?" said Bart.

Foote nodded. The wind kicked up and Foote shivered. Du Pré took off his worn stained leather jacket and handed it to him. Foote put it on.

"Damn," said Bart, "He's close to looking human."

"Come on," said Jeanne, taking Foote's arm, "You are a pitiful tightass white but we be as nice to you as we can. Long bus trip."

Foote smiled at Bart, Madelaine, Du Pré. He went off with Jeanne toward the bus.

"Him, he knew," said Madelaine.

"Yup," said Bart, "Good sport about it though."

"You," said Madelaine, "Maybe you better not say that yet."

Foote and Jeanne went up the bus steps and the door closed and the engine whined and the buses took off.

"Charles," said Bart, "is a good man."

"Very smart," said Madelaine.

"Ver' ver' smart," said Du Pré.

"He will track us all down," said Bart.

Du Pré nodded.

He began to whistle "Billy Drank the Gold."